"My Name Is Keely Donovan. Will You Be My Mommy?"

Quinn's daughter asked, tugging on Taylor's hand.

"Keely!" he said sharply.

Unused to her father's admonishing tone, Keely rounded her eyes, her bottom lip trembling as she looked up at him. "But, Daddy, we don't have one. You said that we couldn't have ladies who wore wedding rings. She isn't, so can we have her?"

Taylor wrapped Keely's hand firmly in hers. The icy expression she lifted to Quinn challenged him. "I am certain that Keely is only voicing an honest request. She's trying to help you, though it is abundantly clear to me why the position is vacant."

Dear Reader,

It's summer. The days are longer and they sure are *hotter*. But it's not just the temperature that's heating up…it's also the magnificent men of Silhouette Desire.

This month, we're bringing you six hunky heroes who are so cute, we think they're "Centerfolds." And we've put each of them on the cover, so you can see—*very* up-close and personal—just how handsome these magnificent specimens of manhood really are.

Their stories are brought to you by some of your favorite writers, beginning with a super-sexy *Man of the Month* book, *Fusion,* by Cait London. The sizzle continues with hot romances by Merline Lovelace (whose name you might recognize from her Harlequin Historicals), Naomi Horton, Rita Rainville (who proves sexy can also be funny), Barbara McCauley and Susan Carroll.

So if you want to stay cool—stay by the air conditioner! But if you want some sizzle in your summer, reach for these Centerfolds!

Until next month—happy reading from

Lucia Macro
Senior Editor

Please address questions and book requests to:
Silhouette Reader Service
U.S.: 3010 Walden Ave., P.O. Box 1325, Buffalo, NY 14269
Canadian: P.O. Box 609, Fort Erie, Ont. L2A 5X3

CAIT LONDON
FUSION

SILHOUETTE *Desire*
Published by Silhouette Books
America's Publisher of Contemporary Romance

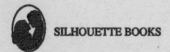 SILHOUETTE BOOKS

ISBN 0-373-05871-3

FUSION

Copyright © 1994 by Lois Kleinsasser

Books by Cait London

Silhouette Desire

The Loving Season #502
Angel vs. MacLean #593
The Pendragon Virus #611
The Daddy Candidate #641
Midnight Rider #726
The Cowboy #763
Maybe No, Maybe Yes #782
The Seduction of Jake Tallman #811
Fusion #871

Silhouette Books

Spring Fancy 1994
"Lightfoot and Loving"

CAIT LONDON

lives in the Missouri Ozarks but grew up in Washington and still loves craggy mountains and the Pacific Coast. She's a history buff and an avid reader who knows her way around computers. She grew up painting landscapes and wildlife, but is now committed to writing and enjoying her three creative daughters. Cait has big plans for her future—learning to fish, taking short trips for research and meeting people. She also writes as Cait Logan and won the *Romantic Times* Best New Romance Writer award when she first started writing.

Here's to rainbows and dreams, and to Margaret

One

How could the scent of baby powder make him feel so safe? Quinn Donovan wondered. The soft, limp drape of his sleeping daughter's limbs against him held the midnight terror at bay. Freshly bathed and sprinkled with "fairy dust"—otherwise known as baby powder—four-year-old Keely sighed against his throat, her tousled curls catching the breeze from Ferguson Lake. Quinn cuddled her closer, laying his cheek against her soft one, rocking her as he stood in the doorway of the old gristmill that served as their home.

He brought a chubby hand to his mouth and kissed it. Keely was his, a part of his body, his eternity. He'd fight to keep her safe. Just as he'd fight for his parents and cousins and the other residents of Blarney Flats, Arkansas. At thirty-nine, he'd learned that what was worth keeping was worth the fight.

Quinn gently nuzzled Keely's black cap of curls. During the days, Keely's bursts of giggles, her delight in fairy tales and butterflies, filled his heart. Yet he savored the quiet moments at night, holding his daughter against him.

When she was safe, and his alone.

The old mill settled for the night, the waterwheel still, the millpond's water trickling by, unused.

He rocked Keely, bracing his legs against the hundred-and-twenty-five-year-old floor of the gristmill. Out on Ferguson Lake, Sir Elmo, a giant bullfrog, bellowed his supremacy from a lily pad. According to local legends, a new baby Loch Ness monster nestled in the very deepest waters. Fireflies skirted the stream leading from the lake to the millpond, and tree frogs sang in the night.

Quinn frowned, thinking of Maudie Culpepper's heir, Taylor Hart. With a scrawl of his pen, Hart could destroy the safety of the small community.

"Not in my lifetime," Quinn promised darkly, kissing Keely's cheek. He'd failed at his dreams, and watched a career he'd forged crash to the ground. Quinn closed his eyes, remembering the rubble of the unfinished, poorly constructed office building. As an up-and-coming New York architect, he'd tried a unique design and babied it into reality. When it collapsed, the destruction had nearly cost lives. The fault was his.

All his fine dreams had fallen with the building, and the last shreds of his marriage. He forced away the memory of Keely's mother shaking her viciously when she was two months old. Then there were more nightmares before Nancy had signed over custody of the baby to Quinn.

He'd taken his baby to Blarney Flats, to his family, where Keely would be loved and protected, surrounded by doting grandparents and teasing cousins.

He inhaled the scents of the night, honeysuckle mixed with freshly tilled earth and newly cut grass.

If Taylor Hart sold or developed Maudie's land and her small natural lake, Blarney Flats could die.

"Hart will have a fight on his hands," Quinn whispered, nuzzling Keely's cheek and thinking of the surveyors and land developers who had been circling the Culpepper property in the past four months.

* * *

The next morning, Quinn jabbed the brush into the gingerbread trim's pink paint. If Taylor Hart endangered Blarney, he would have to answer to one Quinn Donovan.

The late-May morning lingered in the dew on Maudie's overgrown rose garden, where Keely served tea to her dolls. The Victorian-style two-story house, with its angular, jutting roofs and wide front porch, was very different from Quinn's bare living quarters over Blarney's gristmill.

Keely loved playing in the gardens and on the spacious front porch while Quinn repainted the house in Maudie's favorite shade of powder blue. He'd also restored missing sections of the gingerbread trim, and had just begun to paint it this morning.

Quinn dipped the brush into the pink paint and stroked along the intricate decorative molding. He enjoyed the sun on his bare back, while he angled his six-foot-four body across the roof's sharp ridge. Lying on top of the wooden shingle roof—the best way to paint the high gingerbread trim on Maudie's old house—Quinn surveyed Blarney's single downtown street and traced its ambling path up the hill to Hummingbird Lane.

Keely was a favored child of the elderly people who lived along Hummingbird Lane—especially Maudie Culpepper. Small, spritely Maudie, with her collection of teapots and her beautiful antique furniture, had asked Quinn to paint and repair her home just before she passed away in January.

Little was known about Maudie, except that she had owned Ferguson Lake, which lay behind her house. The lake and the surrounding thousand acres had been a bridal gift from her husband, Samuel, the last Culpepper in Blarney Flats. Her family had visited twice, carrying with them a chill and a snobbish arrogance. "Poor dear Maudie," the townsfolk had whispered.

Everyone wondered when Taylor Hart, the sole person to inherit Maudie's estate, would arrive...and exactly what he would do with Ferguson Lake.

"Daddy? Do you think I can catch a leprechaun today?" Keely called up to Quinn as she cradled her favorite doll, Queenie. "If I do, I won't ask for the pot of gold at the end of the rainbow. I'll ask for my very own mommy."

Quinn thought fleetingly of Nancy's betrayal in their business and in their bed. He thought of the disastrous end of their marriage and Nancy trading Keely to him. She was his daughter alone now and believed her mother had "gone to heaven." However, Nancy remained alive and the custody papers said she would never come close to Keely again. One day he'd find a way to tell Keely the truth....

Quinn grinned down at her. "Poor me. How would I manage, a poor man pitted against two fairy princesses? A man wants meat and potatoes, not fairy dew and leprechaun cookies."

Keely giggled delightedly, her black curls bouncing. Keely held Queenie and performed a jig that could entrance the coldest heart—if there were any in Blarney Flats.

Warm hearts. Cows grazing in the meadows. Twelve-year-old Danny O'Day's famed shamrock-green kites flying in the breeze. Keely would be safe here, wrapped in love.

In the valley below, morning shadows and mist clung to Blarney's one street. Quinn watched from the rooftop as metal glinted in the fog and an expensive-looking gray rental car slid up the hill to stop in front of Maudie's white picket fence. A tall, slender woman with black hair knotted on top of her head stepped from the car. Dressed in a classic gray business pantsuit, a white blouse and carrying a bulging, worn leather briefcase, the woman stood still on the sidewalk. Around shielding sunglasses, milky skin covered aristocratic cheekbones. From his viewpoint, Quinn glimpsed a firm mouth and hollowed cheeks.

The woman firmly pushed open the gate of the white picket fence and strode up the walkway. She stopped a few feet from the front porch, slashing impatient assessing glances at the flower and herb gardens and at Ferguson Lake, lying behind the house.

In the shadows, her body shifted restlessly on her long legs. She slowly lifted her face to him, her stylish sunglasses glinting like round twin mirrors. "Who are you, and what are you doing on my property?"

"*Your* property?" Quinn asked warily, skimming the restless feminine body in the stylish loose gray suit. He let the thought sink in and turned it over slowly. So Taylor Hart had sold Maudie's property quickly. "Are you representing Taylor Hart?"

"I *am* Taylor Hart."

"You're a woman," he said flatly. Quinn had prepared to deal with a man...perhaps take him fishing, let him see the beauty that was Blarney. This woman, brisk and all business, was another matter.

Her jaw angled defiantly. "So it seems," she said sharply. "Do you have a problem with that? Oh, I see. You were prepared to deal with a man. Doing business, or trying to do business, with a woman intimidates you."

The carefully spaced words challenged Quinn's peaceful morning. So this was Taylor Hart. A woman who spoke her name as if she were the high ladyship expecting bows from underlings. "Quinn Donovan," he replied, annoyed by her tone.

Few men or women had jerked Quinn's temper, but those who had knew what lay on the far side of his charm. Quinn didn't like revealing his dark side, and few had drawn it from him.

"Taylor Hart. Feminine gender," the woman clarified crisply. Then, "Don't tell me my great-aunt Maudie's house comes with a painting gargoyle on the rooftop," she snapped, sidestepping a pink drop that fell from his brush. It splattered her gray business pumps. When her sunglasses lasered up to him, the tight knot on top of her head shone blue-black in the sunlight shafting through Maudie's maple tree.

Quinn's stomach tightened. At this moment, Taylor Hart—female—wore trouble like some women wore lipstick—smooth, glossy, and dangerous. Taylor Hart riffled

Quinn's pleasant morning like a storm's wind tossing waves
on a lake.

When he met her stare, refusing to give more than she did,
the woman pushed her sunglasses to the top of her head.
"You must be the handyman Aunt Maudie hired. I'm her
great-niece and heir. I own this place now, and I won't be
needing your services."

Quinn pushed his lips into a smile. "I promised Maudie
that her house would look its best—for *you*, Taylor Hart,"
he said, too gently, smugly.

The woman shifted her weight, slashing out an impatient
hand at her side. "I see. Well, I don't want to waste time
over this. You can keep whatever she paid you in advance.
But if you don't leave in the next five minutes, I'll have the
local law serve up a trespassing warrant."

Quinn thought of Moriarity, the local sheriff and judge,
his cousin twice removed. No one was ever arrested in Blarney except on Saint Patrick's Day, and then only for the
major crime of not wearing green. Moriarity's grandmother had claimed that the grain Quinn milled for her was
the finest ever, and that she would curse anyone who of-
fended him. Moriarity's wife wanted Quinn to refinish her
great-grandmother's dowry chest. It sat in his workroom at
the mill now, waiting to be stripped and tightened. "Do
what you must do," he invited quietly, nudging aside the
disquieting ripple the woman had caused in his peace.

Then he took a long look at her legs and wondered how
she would look beneath him.

The thought hit Quinn broadside, winding him. Then a
second thought swept away the first, as he wondered how
her hair would look loose around her shoulders. Quinn
jabbed the brush into the paint, crediting his thoughts to
sleepless nights and nightmares.

Taylor scanned the blue house intently, a woman set on
her course—to dissect it, and calculate its dollar value.
"Ghastly colors. Old houses are always white."

"Look around," he invited, swirling the brush along the
gingerbread molding. The woman glanced up and down

Hummingbird Lane, a cobblestone street lined with magnificent old houses of every color, with their sprawling
porches and gardens.

"Fine. I know that backwoods Arkansas moves in a different time zone, but I don't have time or patience to debate anything, especially not with a handyman," Taylor
said, anger trimming her low, husky tones. Her frown
swung up, pinning him. "Get off that roof and off my
property. *Now.*"

Quinn noted with satisfaction that her knuckles whit-
ened as she gripped her briefcase. "Lady, you must have
gotten up on the wrong side of the bed," he said slowly, and
wondered who was loving her in the early-morning hours.

Then Keely moved into the arena of their silent war. She
tugged at the woman's hand, looking up at her. "My name
is Keely Donovan. Will you be my mommy?"

"Keely!" Quinn knew he had spoken too sharply the
moment his daughter's name left his lips.

Unused to the admonishing tone, she looked up at him,
her eyes round, her bottom lip trembling. Tears shimmered
in the catwillow green eyes matching his own. "But, Daddy,
we don't have one," she stated unsteadily. "You said that we
couldn't have ladies who wore wedding rings. She isn't, so
can we have her?"

Taylor Hart-woman wrapped Keely's hand firmly in hers.
The icy expression she lifted to Quinn challenged him. "I
am certain that Keely is only voicing an honest request. She's
trying to help you, though it is clear to me why the position
is vacant."

Quinn inhaled and pressed his lips closed. With Keely's
eyes round and her bottom lip trembling, setting Taylor
Hart straight would have to wait.

"The wrong side of the bed, my foot!" Taylor muttered
as she entered the house, noting absently that the door was
unlocked. Donovan could distract and charm his daughter
with a dazzling grin and an offer of ice cream, but he still
wasn't wanted on the premises. Taylor didn't like the quick

slash of anger in his dark eyes or the set of his jaw when
she'd told him to leave. The wind had caught his shoulder-
length hair, lifting it away from his dark skin, reminding her
of a warlock defending his lair. The folded red bandanna
across his brow had emphasized the lashing contempt of his
deep-set eyes.

The air had sizzled between them, steaming with heavy
silence. Now, with the sun at his back, she couldn't see
Donovan properly through the parlor window, but she
caught the sheen of perspiration on his jutting cheekbones,
and the taut cord of muscle running down his jaw. She
traced the sound of footsteps across the roof. A ladder
creaked and beyond the lacy white curtains, Quinn Donovan's tall, lean body struck the ground like a javelin, worn
running shoes first. Deep black waves of hair flowed down
the back of his neck. His back and arms rippled as he
scooped up his daughter and tossed her into the air. The
closed windows muffled a masculine chuckle and a childish
squeal of delight. Donovan locked his legs apart, the worn
jeans molding his taut backside before flowing over long,
long legs.

Taylor tightened her lips, crossing her arms. While Donovan's daughter was dressed in a pretty ruffled yellow sun-
dress, the father's clothing—what there was of it—was
worn, faded in obvious places and sagged low on his hips.
The hole on his upper thigh was dangerously revealing,
showing the bottom of an inside pocket; a gaping hole low
on the back of his thigh exposed dark, hair-flecked skin.

The little girl—Keely—wrapped her arms around her
father's broad shoulders. She smacked him with a juicy kiss,
tucked a daisy over his ear and grinned. Donovan smiled,
said something, then buried his face in her neck. There were
rumbling, growling noises that raised the hair on the back
of Taylor's neck. Delighted by her father's play, Keely wiggled and squealed with laughter.

Clearly, Donovan knew how to manage his mommy-
hunting daughter.

The pain of forgotten memories ricocheted through Taylor before she pushed it back into its familiar hole. She latched the mental gate with a skill born of practice.

Then, beneath the rolled red bandanna across his brow, Donovan's fierce scowl shot through the lacy curtains to scald her, jerking her from the weak moment. The sun gleamed on the tight skin covering his cheekbones, and his eyes flashed in the shadows cast by thick brows and lashes. Donovan held the girl protectively, wrapping her against him with strong, pink-spattered arms before lifting her to straddle his bare shoulders. He shot Taylor another fierce warning, then strode away as if sweeping his daughter to safety.

"Barbarian," Taylor muttered, tugging her gaze away from that tapered, muscled back and those low slung jeans. She forced herself to dismiss the irritation that was Donovan. Six days at Maudie's left little time to deal with anything.

Taylor was deeply exhausted from business—and the trip from Chicago. She'd missed a connecting flight and decided to rent a car and drive the rest of the way to Blarney Flats, commonly called Blarney.

"Not that it's his problem, but I did get up on the wrong side of the bed. A very lumpy bed," Taylor admitted to a teapot that looked like a hippopotamus. She scanned the green, rolling Arkansas hills quickly, her body tense. Determined to arrive at her aunt's home quickly, Taylor had bypassed lovely bed-and-breakfast places along the winding rural highway. When she almost fell asleep at the wheel, she'd decided to take whatever lodging came next.

The Last Hawg Café and Motel had been as bad as its name. Her first night in an Arkansas motel hadn't been a highlight of her life. Good old boys dressed in plaid shirts and dirty jeans—the "How-'bout-it-babe?" sort—infested the roadside café and motel. Spiked with various belching contests, which carried through the paper-thin walls, the beer party in the next room had continued until dawn. The motel had finally fallen silent then, but Taylor had had enough, and she'd left an hour later.

To worsen her mood, she'd discovered that a beautiful, well-kept bed and breakfast lay just one mile from the Last Hawg.

She wrapped her arms around herself and surveyed her great-aunt's home. Daylight, muted by the lacy curtains, settled on the sheets and dustcovers in the parlor. Taylor carefully eased aside a ruffled, starched doily to place the briefcase containing her computer and her files on an old pedestal table. "Oh, Aunt Maudie..." she whispered to the shadows.

Taylor's family said Aunt Maudie was "unique," "un-usual" and "interesting." That meant she didn't follow the Hart business-and-profits-or-die mold. Sixty-five years ago, Maudie had followed her heart and married a man without an education. A graduate cum laude of an elite college, and the black sheep of the Hart family, Maudie had returned from a sight-seeing trip in Arkansas and declared that she was marrying a man she'd fallen in love with at first sight. Her father—Taylor's great-great grandfather, and a Yan-kee carpetbagger, if the truth be known—had promptly disinherited Maudie. Her name had never again been men-tioned in his presence.

When Taylor's great-aunt Cecilia passed away, Taylor had inherited her journals, which mourned her sister, Maudie. On a whim, Taylor had written to Great-aunt Maudie. The resulting warm note was scripted elegantly, and had arrived with a sprig of lavender. It was an invitation to visit that Taylor had never found time to accept, though she had en-joyed writing to her aunt.

Aunt Maudie's letters had a sense of timelessness, of warmth and home. There was a balance of reality, charm and dreams and always love. Along with the rest of her el-derly peers, Aunt Maudie had loved Blarney Flats and fret-ted about the blight on her roses and the farmers' crops. The ladies' tea circle had admired her collection of teapots and china cups and saucers, which Taylor had added to frequently.

Taylor slowly drew away the dustcovers in the parlor. The elegance and warmth of the 1880s flowed through the room. A china teapot and cups sat in the center of the round pedestal table. Propped against the rose-blossom-shaped teapot was a small white envelope. "Taylor," Aunt Maudie had written, a slight tremor in her elegant, slanting script.

With trembling fingers, Taylor slid the note from the lavender-scented envelope. "Hello, Taylor," Maudie had written.

I'll be gone when you read this. I'm sorry I missed you and that we never actually met, but I feel I know you just the same. There are things that will need tending after I'm gone, and you are just the lovely person to take care of everything. The roses, my Samuel's beautiful furniture, and most of all the people, because they are mine, just as surely as if I'd had children. Love them for me, won't you? You'll do what's best, I know. That makes the going easy.

I love you, Taylor. Never forget love, my dear, because love is magic. The Flynns and the Donovans say it's the work of the fairies, the good ones. Whatever you do, make time for love. I've never regretted loving Samuel, nor disobeying my father. That is what I would wish for you, my dearest Taylor. Love. I've been happy here. You could be, too. Remember that.

Your Aunt Maudie

Taylor placed the note over her rapidly beating heart and walked slowly through the downstairs rooms. Tinted with the promise of summer, May spilled into the house, the scents of lavender and roses and love drifting through the shadows and sunshine. A bouquet of dried pink rosebuds filled a blue antique vase, and the sturdy ornate 1880s furniture was covered with doilies and gold-framed photographs. A china cabinet with claw feet held teapots and cups and saucers, sugar bowls, and cut-glass spoon holders. Taylor placed her palm over the smooth glass, letting the delicate bygone beauty swirl around her.

Yellow accents skipped merrily throughout the old-fashioned kitchen. Like the other rooms, it was covered with flowery wallpaper. The spacious room was cluttered with cooking utensils, dried herbs hanging by the window, spice racks on the walls. Tattered cookbooks filled with notations and clipped recipes lay on a table with an assortment of unopened mail dated after Maudie's passing. Quinn Donovan's business card, which read Miller, Carpenter, Furniture Restoration and listed an address and telephone number, was tucked on top of the mail.

Taylor stirred the dried petals and leaves in an elegant shallow bowl, and a delicate fragrance—roses and lemons—filled the room. A small, gloomy collection of medicine bottles and pill vials sat near a can decorated with glued paper and shell macaroni. Keely's name, written in a childish scrawl in red crayon, rambled over the paper.

Taylor's fingertip brushed the can, and she fought the sudden surge of emotion rising within her.

How she had wanted her baby. How she would have loved—

She jerked her finger away from the can and curled her hand into a fist, locking it against her side. She closed her eyes and willed away the pain that rarely escaped her leash.

The next instant, Taylor turned, gripped the smoothly polished walnut banister like a lifeline and surged up the stairs. She had a job to do, and she would do it the best way she knew how.

The two bedrooms were just like the downstairs—Maudie's house was well kept, but packed with years' worth of furniture, doilies and keepsakes. Glancing at the ticking clock beside Maudie's bed, Taylor noted that she had spent four hours wandering through the house.

She slowly descended the stairs, her hand trailing on the elegant, timeworn curved banister. She continued to touch here and there, absorbing the nuances of a woman she'd never met. Screened against insects, Maudie's back porch held a folded cot, a wooden table and two chairs.

The screen door creaked when Taylor opened it to wander down the rock walkway. A push mower rested in the shade by the redwood picnic table. An old-fashioned wooden lawn chair sat overlooking the clear blue lake glistening in the morning sun.

Drawn to the chair, Taylor sat slowly and watched an orange butterfly meander around the garden, then perch on a brass sundial. Birds sang in the distance, and the sun warmed her. Drowsy, Taylor leaned her head back against the chair and closed her eyes. She realized then that she was still clutching Maudie's note, and that whatever time or effort was needed, she would carefully tend Maudie's lifelong possessions.

"Oh, Aunt Maudie, how I wish I'd met you," Taylor murmured as she stood and stretched her arms high, rolling her taut neck. She eased the pins from her hair, winnowing her fingers through it as she inhaled the fresh scents of the spring afternoon. "I'll do my best."

Stepping from her shoes, Taylor wiggled her stocking-clad toes in the cool grass, the freshly cut scent rising like perfume around her. On an impulse, she stripped off her jacket and tossed it to the chair, following it with her ankle-length hose.

The grass was lush between her toes. After Maudie's attorney belatedly notified her of Maudie's death and the inheritance, Taylor had decided she would tend to the matter personally. She'd been in steady motion for one month, scratching time away from her busy schedule as CEO of Winscott Incorporated. Working overtime and catching naps on office couches had taken their toll. Taylor slid her watch from her wrist, dropped it in her pocket and chafed the reddened skin. She'd tightened the band to allow for her recent weight loss. Running on coffee and little else for the past few weeks had left her drained and tense.

The breeze from the lake slid along her body, catching her silky blouse and stroking it against her like a lover's caress.

She'd stopped wearing a bra when she hadn't had time to shop for a new size, deciding instead to use a light camisole. In her lifetime, she'd always dressed very precisely, wearing lingerie to suit business clothing, and she enjoyed the newfound freedom from restriction. Lifting, stretching her arms, she allowed her hair to catch the wind. She closed her eyes, giving herself over to the freedom.

A twig snapped. The hair on the nape of her neck lifted, and the slight breeze stilled for a heartbeat.

"Yes?" she asked, more harshly than she intended, turning to the man in the early-afternoon shadows. Quinn Donovan stood, long legs braced apart, his shoulders filling his open white shirt. Caught at the back of his neck, his long hair gleamed in a bit of sun shooting through the leaves of the big oak tree. His shirtsleeves were rolled back, exposing forearms lightly sprinkled with black hair.

When he placed a thermos on the wooden picnic table, Taylor suddenly sensed that Quinn was a deliberate man. His long fingers slid slowly away from the thermos, and the movement reminded Taylor of a caress. His gaze ran down her body, lingering, touching, seeking, and something within her stirred and grew taut.

"My mother sent potato soup. She's worried you'll have a poor picture of the people hereabouts."

Taylor pressed her lips together, sensing that Donovan's low voice shielded his real thoughts. She shifted uneasily, disliking the leaping sense of awareness in her body, uncomfortable with his eyes watching her carefully. "The thought was nice, but I can find a restaurant."

He took a few steps nearer, and Taylor found her hand locked to the back of the chair. Donovan topped her five-foot-ten-inch height by half a foot. His broad shoulders, narrow hips, and his carelessly combed hair only served to enhance his raw masculinity. He'd discarded the red bandanna tied around his forehead, and his black brows and lashes gleamed in the sun, shadowing his jutting cheekbones. His eyes caught hers—a curiously dark shade of green that matched his daughter's. His dark skin gleamed as it crossed his cheekbones and his jaw; a tiny fresh cut lay along his jaw, as though he'd just shaved.

Taylor jerked her eyes away from the grim set of his mouth. Despite his apparent dark mood, Donovan's mouth was beautiful, sensuous, and her heart quivered and flip-flopped just once. There was a beauty about Donovan, a raw male look—an arrogance, a certainty—and beneath it lay a fine, grim anger that startled her.

Taylor shifted her weight impatiently. Few men could intimidate her, and she disliked the sense that this man—this Quinn Donovan—knew exactly what she was thinking. Despite her resolve not to give him another inch, when Donovan took another step toward her, she released the chair and stepped backward.

A quick flare of satisfaction soared through Donovan's narrowed eyes, and Taylor's throat tightened.

She straightened her shoulders. She refused to be intimidated by a towering bully. She caught his scent—soap, freshly cut wood, sweat, and a dark, masculine tang that she knew she'd remember forever.

Taylor stepped back again, then regretted the action. Donovan was hunting her now. The dark meadow green eyes skimmed her mussed hair, the loose, untucked blouse open at her throat, catching the fast beat of her heart, then flowing down her body to linger on bare toes locked in the grass.

The heat of his body snared her; his inspection of her feet too intimate.

"I haven't invited you to spoil my day. Creeping up on me this way is trespassing."

"I don't creep." Donovan's flat statement cut into the clean spring air.

His voice reminded her of the rumble of a storm, of a dark beast rising from his lair. From his narrowed eyes came the glittering thrust of a sword, raised and waiting.

Taylor shifted restlessly. She didn't like being questioned or intimidated by a man who could clearly throw her down on the lush grass and... She pushed back the thought of

Donovan's big body lying over hers. Given his arrogance, his raw beauty, he'd probably helped himself to enough willing women. Taylor's friend, Lacey, would have sighed, "Dish... Hunk..."

Donovan's looks were just the sort to be found on a beef-cake calendar—a heated look from those hard green eyes, that tuft of hair curling from his opened shirt widened to expose a broad, darkly tanned chest, perhaps with the snap of his jeans unopened... Taylor pushed back that thought.

"You are trespassing, and you crept up on me," she tossed back at him.

He moved slowly, reaching to lift a curl from her shoulder. He played with the tip, studying the colors. An expert at keeping people emotionally distanced from her, Taylor stared at him coolly and waited for him to step back. But he didn't move away.

"Well now, Taylor Hart, I reckon that's the first time anyone has ever used those words to me. As for the creeping part, *anyone* could have heard me. Except someone who was deep in thought—like you. As for the trespassing... I have business here."

The drawl stilled the trembling air, the heat rising between them. Taylor refused to give Donovan the pleasure of knowing her unease, her sense that she should run and never look back.

Taylor squared her shoulders. She'd never run from anything in her life. "What do you want?"

Donovan's eyes flickered, his gaze drifting over her face, touching her mouth, her cheeks, and settling on her eyes.

She didn't trust what lurked behind that dark emerald stare, any more than she trusted the unsteady beating of her heart.

"For one thing, there's the fixing and painting I promised Maudie would be done to put the place in tip-top shape for her heir. The second reason I'm here is to talk with you."

"Make it fast," she shot back, color rising in her cheeks, the stance of her body taut, challenging.

Two

Fast. Quinn lingered momentarily over the thought that a woman like Taylor was not to be experienced quickly.

The passion rising in her quivered between them, taunting him, making him hungry for the taste of her mouth against his skin. She moved restlessly, her smoky blue eyes locked fearlessly with his.

The breeze caught her fragrance, tangling him in scents. Quinn sorted soap from the natural feminine scents. Beneath the hint of cool subtlety ran a tantalizing, exotic scent that spoke of heat and passion.

Quinn fought the heavy thudding of his body, fought the need to take that furious mouth beneath his. Her reaction to him, the flickering awareness, the nervous lift of her hand to draw her unbuttoned collar together, pleased him. Why?

Taylor was cut from the same mold as Nancy. Tough, heartless businesswomen, rushing through life, acquiring accounts to hoard away. What was he doing, drooling after this woman?

He'd lost his dreams, his soul, to a woman exactly like this one. Taylor had strolled into his world from one he had locked away. A world he didn't want harming his daughter. The first year after he'd returned to Blarney, Keely was everything. Rebuilding the old miller's living quarters and caring for his daughter's needs kept him too tired to think. He didn't want to think then, to remember anything from his dead career.

He willed himself to think instead of warm, soft women. None came to his mind.

Taylor's pale, slender toes slid into her pumps. He glimpsed a trim ankle, and knew he could circle it with his fingers.

Quinn's hand curled tightly. He'd had one go 'round with a woman like this, and nothing could make him step into that cold, painful pit again. He focused on Taylor's threat to Blarney. "What are you planning to do with Maudie's estate?"

"Sell it, of course." The return was flat. "Now that you know what I intend, you may go."

The high-and-mighty tone speared inside Quinn, nettling him instantly. "You're a mite prickly, aren't you, lady?" he drawled, resenting the way she could raise his hackles and his accent.

There was a time when he'd been ashamed of his background, of his upbringing. Fresh from Blarney Flats, a rangy college graduate from "the sticks," he'd practiced dropping his *mite pricklys* and picking up his *ings*.

She angled her face up to him, the sky dropping into her eyes. Or was it the clear lake that made her eyes so blue? Quinn wondered.

Rigid in her anger, Taylor Hart wasn't a classically beautiful woman. Widely spaced dark blue eyes pinned his; black hair raked by the wind crossed her pale forehead and slid across those smooth cheeks. Like gleaming silk ribbons, the long strands rippled on her white throat and flew away into the wind. The set of her jaw was strong, clean. Quinn's gaze caught dimples lurking beside her tightly pressed mouth, and he wondered if her lips had tasted smiles in this lifetime.

Fine lines of fatigue framed her mouth and eyes, and the darkness beneath her eyes served to make them more stormy. She was fierce, he decided, and lonely, like a boat without a mooring. Perhaps that was why he wanted to take her in his arms and hold her close.

Quinn studied that mouth and decided in an instant that he would taste its softness before their moment was over.

When she moved, her breast brushed his arm, and everything within Quinn stilled, centered on that softness. *How long had it been since a woman's breast filled his hand?*

Too long, his body said, taunting him.

He'd thought that when his body jerked to sexual life again, the needs rising after years, the woman arousing him would be lush and soft. But Taylor's body would be streamlined, her breasts mounding gently. A willowy waist led into trim, girlish hips that would barely fill a man's hands.

"I'm not ready to go just yet, Tay," he drawled, turning away from her to face the lake. His reaction to the woman angered him, and anger was a dark emotion he hadn't allowed himself for years.

Taylor chewed on the nickname he'd tossed at her like a bone, just as he'd known she would. The air was vibrating with her anger. The success of his small thrust pleased him. *Were her eyes the color of sky or of blue smoke?*

"If you're the goodwill ambassador of Blarney Flats—I don't know why they call it flat when it's hilly—they're in trouble," Taylor said at his side. Her tone had the low, snarling sound of a tigress gearing up for a mauling, and Quinn waited, letting her set the pace.

Her long, slender fingers flexed once, the practical short nails digging into her thigh.

"Go on," he invited after a moment, flicking her a lazy look that belied the tight, sensual heaviness he was surprised to find in his body.

She sighed—an impatient let's-get-this-over-with sound. "I'm aware that Maudie befriended the town. She loved the town and its people. Although there is a quaint backwoods atmosphere here, I've surveyed the situation and decided that Maudie's property—including the lake—is best sold."

Quinn turned slowly. Taylor's restless pale hands moved to contain the wild, windblown disarray of her hair.

The wind molded her clothing against her, and Quinn's body reacted instantly. He dug his fingers into his palms, wondering how that milky skin would feel beneath his work-roughened hands.

Like cool silk. Her scents swirled around him, and Quinn dived into them greedily.

She shifted her weight, like a cat twitching its tail before pouncing. She lifted her head, her smoky eyes meeting his. "I'll be here exactly six days, Donovan. Stay out of my way and off the premises. And you will not call me 'Tay' again."

Not a man to be dismissed easily, Quinn thought of taking that sassy, grim mouth and leaving her with the taste of him on her lips. Taylor would be calling on him and on his terms soon enough. "I'll be finishing the work I promised Maudie—when it suits me," he murmured easily, taking his time leaving. "Be sure you taste the soup, Tay. From the looks of you, you need the nourishment."

"Why Quinn Donovan?" Taylor muttered at nine o'clock that night, searching for the same man she had chased off her property earlier. She flipped the thought over. Donovan had the look of a man who would fight for what he wanted, not a man to easily chase away. He'd left because it suited him.

Quinn Donovan. The last she'd seen of him was him walking away from her. Swaggering—she corrected, Donovan swaggered. An untamed-male, here-I-am-ladies swagger.

Donovan had left her spoiling for a fight, picking his moment with a simple, "Fine."

A nap on Aunt Maudie's big brass bed hadn't trimmed her memory of Quinn's arrogance. Drained by fatigue and seduced by the smells of freshly cut grass floating in the open window and the gentle flow of curtains lifted by the breeze, Taylor had slept deeply on the washed-soft, hand-stitched quilt. When she awakened, she'd discovered the lack of electricity and a telephone. She'd decided to stretch her tense muscles by walking to the nearest restaurant and seeking out the whereabouts of the small community's local fix-it man.

Blarney Flats was quiet. A mist floated over the cobblestones of its only street, gleaming in the lamplight. Dampness settled on Taylor's skin and in her loose hair, drawing the strands into spiraling curls. Since she would never see these people again, Taylor allowed the wanton gypsy look.

She had flagged down the passing police car bumping along on the cobblestones—if a mud-splattered, dented pickup with overhead lights and a sheriff's badge painted on the side could be called a patrol car. The beefy sheriff had lifted an eyebrow when she queried him about electricity and telephone service, which she would need in the morning. The sheriff's eyes had twinkled, the laughter lines around them deepening. "Quinn Donovan," he'd said with laughter in his slow drawl. "He's in the pub now."

Taylor inhaled once, scowled at the row of frolicking leprechauns painted on the pub's window, then hit the scarred brass shamrock on the heavy door and pushed.

The tavern was what she'd expected—a bar, booths and tables for those who wished to eat. She'd stopped in a thousand places just like this when she traveled and found that the food was usually uncommonly good. The aromas tantalized her, and her stomach clenched as she tried to remember the last time she ate. Country music blared from a jukebox, men and women in the single room were dressed in jeans and boots, and two couples were testing country steps on the small dance floor. In the shadows, Donovan, boots up on a table, cradled a mug of foam-topped beer on his flat stomach.

Taylor picked her way through the tables, and Quinn's
dark brooding stare followed her. She refused to smooth her
wrinkled jacket or her rioting hair, refused to give Donovan any impression that he caused her to be skittish. She
stopped in front of his table; she refused to grimace at the
sight of his well-worn western boots, crossed at the ankle
and resting on the scarred table. "Donovan. I'm without a
telephone and electricity," she stated, noting the pink
slashes of paint on his faded jeans. She jerked her eyes away
from the tattered holes in the denim covering her thighs an
the dark flesh beneath it. His white shirt was unbuttoned
almost to the waist, and the dim light caught in the black
hair covering his chest.

Her mouth dried instantly, and she shivered just once.
Donovan's hard mouth softened as though flirting with a
quick smile, then stilled.

"So?" The taunting drawl was what she had expected.
Donovan lifted one eyebrow, like a king holding court, or
rather, the supreme here-I-am-ladies male waiting for the
candidates of the evening.

Taylor's hand curled into a fist. She wasn't used to asking favors, but the sheriff had informed her that the best
electrician in town was Donovan. Donovan alone had been
granted the privilege of connecting and disconnecting telephone service. And the Mr. Fix-It of Blarney Flats was
making her do the running. "I'll make it worth your time—
your overtime," Taylor said tightly. "I need electricity and
the telephone for business in the morning. I'll need a lock or
the doors, too."

She refused to mention the tiny pink bow caught in
Quinn's black waves. Lodged behind his ear, the shabbily
tied affair only heightened his rakish pirate-overlord air. No
doubt tied as a marker of some steamy tryst. Taylor shook
aside the thought. She didn't care how magnificently Donovan would steam in a tryst.

"Ah!" he said knowingly, dark green eyes gleaming like
those of a warlock who has forced his prey to enter his lair.
"So you've come to me, Tay. The last time we met, you were

hrowing me off *your* property. There were words like *tres-
assing* and *creeping* thrown around." He rocked lazily on
he back legs of his chair, studying her. "So now you've
ome for me. You want me."

Taylor locked her eyes with his, refusing to ignite. Don-
van had known he held a pat hand when he walked away
rom her earlier. She grimly tucked that knowledge away for
uture reference. "Will you, or will you not hook up the
tilities?"

Donovan scanned the dancers, playing with the idea as if
e had until eternity. The angle of his jaw said he would take
is time extracting whatever he needed from her. "To-
ight?"

She shifted and inhaled. He was playing with her, and she
oted the way the other patrons were watching with inter-
st. "I'm not in the mood for cat and mouse, Donovan."

"Neither am I, Taylor Hart." His eyes lifted to hers, then
kimmed the damp, spiraling curl bouncing near her cheek.
he gritted her teeth as his gaze traced her ear, and some-
hing inside her jerked, as though his teeth had caught and
ugged at her lobe.

"I'll pay double your usual rate. You can put the locks on
n the morning, but I need the telephone and electricity to-
ight," she tossed at him, anxious to fly into the safety of
he foggy night and away from Quinn's dark inspection.
'I'm sorry about interfering with your beer, but I have a job
nd business to complete in the morning."

She plopped her purse on the table. Donovan's boots re-
nained locked on the surface while she foraged for her bill-
old and jerked out some money.

The worn boots lifted, then hit the floor. Callused, strong
nd warm, his hand closed over hers, jamming the bills back
n her purse. "Not now." Quinn tugged her hand, jerking
er to his side. "I'll do the hookups. For a dance. One
lance," he murmured, his face close to hers.

Taylor hesitated, aware of his thumb stroking the back of
er hand, caressing her. The challenge was there in his eyes,
 dark gleam flickering beneath his lashes.

"Are you afraid?" he asked quietly.

"Of you? Of course not," she returned hotly, blowing aside a curling tendril. "However, this is a first for me—dancing with a local handyman."

"Well, then…" Donovan stood in a lithe movement and drew her against him.

Donovan took her body against his as if he had that right, as if she had placed it in his keeping and nothing could take her away from him at this moment. Taylor released the breath she had been holding and waited for her heart to stop racing. Quinn's large hand opened possessively to span the small of her back; his other hand wrapped around hers and took it behind his back.

He'd showered, the scent of soap swirling around him spiced by a light after-shave. Taylor frowned, discovering the fragrance of baby powder flirting among the tantalizing male scents.

When she stiffened, attempting to draw away, Quinn gathered her closer, until they touched from breast to thigh. "Loosen up, Hart. This won't hurt a bit," he murmured as they moved into a smooth Texas waltz.

The thin pink bow shifted, catching the dim light. Taylor promised herself that she would not ask about that bow. She would not show the slightest interest in him.

"So," Taylor began loftily, nettled by Quinn's experience in holding a woman's body easily, by his assurance that wherever he led, she would follow. "Your daughter is lovely. I hope she has a baby-sitter while you're—"

"Keely is fast asleep now, with a teenage cousin doing her homework in the next room," Quinn returned easily, though his eyes had narrowed challengingly.

"Oh, I see." When Taylor lifted her brows, staring past his shoulder, Quinn twirled her under his arm and brought her close against him. Her body collided against his with a soft breathtaking thud. She fought the sensation of wind, of storms and Quinn's hard body against hers. Muscles thrust at her thighs, pushed against the soft outer sides of her breasts, his leg thrusting intimately between hers as they turned. Without her bra, her breasts were too sensitized, rubbing against his chest.

Taylor forced air into her lungs. Her voice, when it came, was too husky, too tight. "So. This is a frequent pastime for you then—hanging out, drinking beer with your friends..."

His jaw tightened against her temple, the rough skin chafing hers slightly. "If I choose. Today I met a lady with a chip on her shoulder, and I needed to soothe her claw marks."

Taylor turned her head slightly, ready to defend herself, and felt Quinn's warm breath on her lips.

Their eyes locked. He moved against her, testing—his heavy thigh between her legs—and she resisted, challenging his right to her body, her life, the emotions that she didn't want to release. Quinn bent her over his arm, his lips softening sensuously before he stilled them. "Let me go," she ordered furiously, her fingers digging into him, depending upon him to keep her from falling.

She closed her eyes, resenting the loss of control. She'd learned long ago not to depend on anyone.

His hard thighs flexed against hers as he lifted her easily, his eyes marking his victory.

"Throw your orders at your underlings, darlin'. I'm not buying," he returned easily. His hand tightened on hers, keeping her arm wrapped around him. Quinn's lips moved sensuously against her ear. "You're a nervous woman, Taylor Hart. Can't say that I've ever danced with a board."

Quinn's body was warm steel, his jaw slightly rough with evening stubble as it lay against her temple. Taylor kept her neck taut, refusing to yield. "You're too close," she returned, her body edgy, restless, against his. For a woman who preferred her physical space, his close warmth was a trespass. She had a quick image of women draped around Quinn's delectable body, swooning at the dangerous, untamed glint in his dark emerald eyes. "I suppose the locals are waiting to see if their ambassador is making headway. No doubt they've seen you charm and kiss—" Taylor clamped her lips closed, regretting the word the instant it left

her. When she realized her nails were digging into the warm
pad of muscle shifting beneath her hand, she lifted her fin
gers.

"*Kiss*. Now there's an interesting word." The dark, quick
look Quinn shot down heated her. "Do you?" he asked, hi
gaze slipping to her mouth.

"What?" Taylor asked breathlessly as the hand on he
back jerked her slightly against him.

"Kiss well and often?" he shot back.

The question nettled. Taylor didn't allow the demands o
other people to slide beneath her skin, warming it. She'
learned long ago to conceal her emotions.

She eyed him warily, heating at the dark humor she saw
in his eyes. "Donovan, have I paid enough? Is this even
about to finish?" she asked, hoping for a bored tone
though electricity danced along her nerves.

"When it's over."

She lifted her eyebrows. "You're a little old for these
games, aren't you, Donovan?"

"It comes back, now and then," he answered mildly
though there was nothing easy about the way he studied he
mouth.

Taylor looked away. She wanted to run, to fly away from
the danger she found in his eyes, in the taut set of his tal
body against hers. "Everyone is watching," she said warn
ingly.

"They're afraid of you," he murmured, rocking her body
gently against his.

Then there was a long, slow sweep of his open hand down
her spine, pressing her against him. She closed her eyes
fought the safety she sensed lurking in his arms, fought the
danger. She hadn't leaned on anyone for years, needed
anyone.

"That's enough," Quinn said roughly, taking her hand
and dragging her quickly from the pub.

Standing on the cobblestones, Taylor jerked her hand
from his. "Be careful, Donovan. I bite."

Taylor stood in the mists, which glittered in her hair like tiny diamonds, her face pale in the lamplight. Passion shimmered in her, anger mounting, waiting to fly at him. Or was it something else? Quinn wondered, remembering the soft flow of her body against his. When they danced, he had taken her against him hard, resenting his needs and his fears. The soft collision of her body against his, her intimate scents tangling in his senses, had been his undoing.

He'd begun to sweat when he noticed that her breasts were free. The thought drew his body tight, weighted it. When she had moved, her exotic feminine scents wafted up to him, snaring him until he wanted to dive in, wallow in them, taste each one.

Snuggled to him, the firm mounds had shifted, flowing into him, taunting him with his years of restraint. He imagined her teeth biting into his shoulder, the pale undulation of that long feminine body beneath his own. She tossed her magnificent mane away impatiently now and he wondered how it would feel against his bare skin, how she would taste.

What was he doing, thinking about this woman, this streamlined female shark who could rip apart the town's security? What was he doing, acting like the macho jerk she thought he was? *And why the hell did it matter to him what she thought?* "Let's go," he said abruptly, walking away from her.

"Let's go," he repeated curtly when she didn't follow. She stirred his dreams, his passions, and he resented the intrusion. "The sooner you get what you want, the sooner you'll be gone."

"Go? Get back here and fight, you coward." The hiss of a woman burning with temper lashed through the glittering, lamplit mists.

Quinn allowed his smile in the darkness, away from her. He preferred honest rage in a woman; he'd had a bellyful of icy, carefully placed barbs. He'd chipped Taylor's smooth ice a bit, and if nothing else, he'd found out she'd fight when backed into a corner.

He inhaled the damp, soft night, forcing away the thought of the press of breasts against him as they danced, the jut of hips and the warm press of thighs. About two centuries ago, he'd had sex—or rather the cold, unsatisfying shell of it.

His hand locked in a fist. This Hart woman waltzed into his world and started him aching for passion, for the depth and the heat of his body locked in hers. The image winded him, heating his blood. He continued walking away, resenting her, fearing what brewed within himself.

Her purse hit his back, thrown as she snapped, "Look, you...you redneck backwoodsman. The caveman approach is out of date. And by the way, since when do cavemen wear pink bows in their hair?"

Quinn stopped, remembering Keely's bow, and turned slowly. He plucked the small black business purse from the cobblestones. The leather was cool and moist beneath his fingers, a spot warmed here by her hand. He ran his thumb over that warm spot. He knew he was endangering the future of Blarney by treating this woman as he had never treated another. But one glance at her, hands on hips, legs spread on the pavement, as if she'd fight to the end, proved he'd been right about her. Passion nibbled at Taylor Hart's leashes, and whatever passed between them would not be a cold shell. He wanted her then, the heat and the storms swirling around them.

He'd fleetingly wanted other women since Keely's conception, the last time he'd been with a woman. Abstinence from sex had been easy for years before that night and after. Until now.

He walked back to Taylor, enjoying her shimmering uncertainty, the feminine fluttering of her hand along her throat. He wondered then how her skin would taste, how her pulse would feel racing beneath his lips. Taylor flicked her hair back from her shoulder, angling her face up to him in the lamplight.

"Keely was practicing her bows earlier," Quinn explained, then wondered why he felt the need to let Taylor into this part of his life. His daughter's delight when he'd promised he'd wear her first good bow to town wouldn't be shoved aside.

"Oh." She mulled that for a second. Then: "Please tell her that your bow is very pretty. Why are they, the people here, afraid of me?" she asked huskily, impatiently.

Mist tangled in her hair, catching and beading the light, and Quinn thought of a gypsy queen, passionate and tempting. She shivered beneath his gaze, her eyes sliding away.

Maudie Culpepper's great-niece held Blarney by the proverbial throat. Taylor's pale, slender fingers could tear apart Blarney, the town in which Quinn wanted to raise Keely, to keep her safe.

Fascinated by the woman, he dismissed her question. He slid a finger through her hair, letting it curl around him. The damp texture was strong and willful, yet warm, smooth and scented, like the woman. Taylor trembled then, drawing away. "I'll settle my aunt's estate quietly and leave. I don't know what you're after, but intimidating me won't work, Donovan."

Again the lash of her challenge caught him, tantalized him. He settled the curl against the breast of her jacket and stroked it, flattening it against the softness below. A thread of control kept Quinn from jerking her to him. Instead, he touched her again, a stroke of his fingertip along the damp, cool slope of her cheek. Taylor reacted instantly—swatting his hand away and glaring at him. The mist clung and wound around them, heating with Quinn's need to explore. "I'll get my tools," he said, too roughly, concealing the heady excitement stirring within him.

"You're coming then. To connect the telephone and the electricity?" she asked uncertainly.

Quinn nodded, his mood dark, and as unsteady as the mist curling between them. "I have to check on Keely first."

Taylor's glance skimmed by him into the night as the streetlights clicked off. "Ten o'clock," Quinn explained, watching her hands whiten on the black purse. "Blarney closes down at ten on weekdays, midnight on Fridays and Saturdays, and doesn't open on Sundays.''

The bullfrogs and tree frogs began to chorus, and a hoot owl soared past, hunting for a meal. A shadow darted overhead, and Taylor leaned a bit toward him. ''What's that?''

''Ghosts,'' Quinn said, fighting the curling of his lips and feeling half his age.

She swallowed, shot a dark look his way and muttered, ''Very funny.''

Sir Elmo, the biggest bullfrog in Quinn's millpond, bellowed, and Taylor jumped, her eyes widening, skipping into the darkness.

''You could come with me to pick up my tools,'' he offered, expecting her to refuse and half hoping she would come with him.

''I should be going.... I'll meet you at the house.'' The edgy, husky whisper as her eyes darted into the mists covering the night snared him.

''Are you afraid? A woman alone at night?'' he pressed.

She hesitated a moment, turning the thought. ''No, I'm not.''

He pushed away the torment lurking on his tongue, resenting the need to wrap her against him. When she swung away, striding up the hill toward Maudie's, her shoulders squared, Quinn shook his head. He'd seen fright go darting through her eyes when Sir Elmo bellowed, yet she'd turned and met the night alone.

Who took care of Taylor Hart when she cried? he wondered, then damned himself for caring.

Moriarity's pickup bumped along the cobblestones beside Quinn, and the sheriff leaned from the open window. ''Stop leering, old man,'' Quinn said easily, disturbed by his thoughts. ''Follow her home.''

''Whooee, that is a sassy female. Better shut your mouth, boy. Your tongue is hanging out. By the way, boyo—'' Moriarity used the locals' Irish word for *lad* ''—did the lady tell you that your pink hair bow is becoming?''

"You have Flynn blood," Quinn tossed at his cousin easily, reminding him of a Donovan trespass long ago, "or you'd be doing your job instead of gossiping."

Moriarity tipped his battered western hat. "Your moody Russian blood is showing, Quinn. She must be the reason April Dauncey said you looked black as thunder at the pub. The Hart woman has got your dander up, boyo. After living like a monk, you've been broadsided," the sheriff teased before slowly easing the pickup into the mists, following Taylor.

"Barbarian. Creep. Jerk." Taylor flopped on her stomach, rolled the words around in her mouth again, and decided they fit Quinn Donovan perfectly. The brass clock beside Aunt Maudie's bed ticktocked away the minutes after two o'clock in the morning.

Maudie's book, *Care of Scented Geraniums,* hadn't soothed Taylor's need to launch herself at Quinn. Nor had two bowls of Maudie's delicious home-canned peaches.

She had never thrown anything at anyone in her entire lifetime, but when Quinn had swaggered away from her, nothing could have kept her from throwing her purse at him.

Taylor flopped to her back and jammed a pillow behind her neck. Quinn had stormed through the house like a tornado, his flashlight beam running up and down her once before he ordered her out of his way. He'd connected the electricity and the telephone outside the house by stomping over the roof. Then he'd jerked open the door and strode through the house, flicking lights on and off. He'd impatiently tugged at the dial on the old rotary telephone and growled, "Madge, this is an emergency connect. Call back in the morning for billing. I'll vouch for the customer's credit. No...everyone is peachy-keen. Maudie's heir turned up...."

Quinn's black eyes had skipped coldly to Taylor, flicking down her rigid body. "Not a man. A city woman. Yes, she wants to sell.... No, she doesn't know about Ferguson Lake.... Madge, she's standing right here. If you want to know what she's thinking, you can ask her." With that, Quinn had thrust the heavy black receiver at Taylor, then closed the front door behind him.

"This is Madge Colfield, over in Big Toad Junction," the operator's metallic voice had murmured. "Who am I speaking to?"

When Taylor introduced herself, the operator had said quickly, "Quinn must be feeling poorly. He's not usually so snippy. In fact, he's known for his charm and patience. Now, if I can have your name, dear, we'll get the matter of billing out of the way. By the way, you're not thinking of selling Maudie's place to outsiders, are you? Do you know the Flynns and the Donovans are descendants of the Irish who came to this country during the Potato Famine? Please don't think their feud is bitter. Then there's the elderly along Hummingbird Lane, to say nothing of all the wonderful lore that makes Blarney Flats what it is today."

Taylor flopped onto her stomach again as she remembered her body responding to Quinn's. Maudie's bed creaked. Outside, a puppy began yipping excitedly. Unused to sleepless hours and being off her schedule, Taylor resented the weakness now, her thoughts swinging to Quinn. He had kept Keely's bow in his hair, his expression softening as he touched the ribbon. Taylor closed her eyes and saw the sunlight tangling around Quinn as he'd nuzzled his daughter's neck, the girl giggling in his grasp.

Then Taylor saw him bending over her while they danced, forcing her to cling to him for balance, playing games he was much too old for—games *she* had purposely bypassed all her life. Middle age was just a step ahead of her.

Then she thought of Donovan's scent—all male, rugged, darkly exciting. Donovan's mouth would be delicious. What did she know about kissing? Nothing. She seldom kissed babies or friends' cheeks, let alone firm, sensuous lips. She had better things to occupy her time than kissing. Quinn— a man who was almost forty—although a well preserved forty and who should be thinking of getting a profitable career before time ran out. "Just your basic good old boy," she murmured drowsily, clutching the pillow closer and forcing thoughts of Donovan away. At dawn, she inhaled the scents of lavender and sun-dried sheets, and allowed herself to drift away.

Three

———

"I'm cold," a child's voice complained softly beside her. Taylor opened one eye to see Keely standing by the high bed. Keely shyly turned her body from side to side, the brass buckles on her overalls gleaming in the bright morning sun. Her unbrushed hair, and the mismatched buttons on her kitten-patterned blouse, said little for Quinn's caretaking. A white milk circle lurked above her rosebud mouth, and her chin bore an irresistible patch of chocolately crumbs.

Taylor raised up on her elbow and struggled through the layers of sleep. "Keely?"

The little girl placed a chubby finger in Taylor's hair and jerked it back. "Pretty," she said, adding a beguiling grin. "My dolly, Queenie, is cold. She wants to sleep with you." She glanced down at her doll, which was carefully wrapped in a tattered scrap of a blanket, then at Taylor. Heavy footsteps sounded on the roof, and Taylor closed her eyes. Quinn had returned to finish his pink violation of Maudie's gingerbread trim.

With her father on the roof, Keely had been left to her own devices. Taylor jotted a mental note to tell Quinn just what she thought of his parenting abilities. Anything could happen to a wandering, unattended child.

Taylor's fingertips brushed away the crumbs, her hand lingering on Keely's warm, soft cheek. Quinn's daughter was a charmer, smiling like an angel.

Keely's hopeful green eyes melted Taylor's initial resistance. Taylor untangled her legs from the sheets and Maudie's long cotton print nightgown, which she chose to wear instead of her own. She eased aside to make room for Queenie. Keely carefully tucked the worn doll beside Taylor and bent to give Queenie a juicy kiss. She grinned at Taylor, who found herself smiling. "Shhh..." Keely whispered, placing her finger in front of her pursed lips. "The leprechauns don't like to wake up too early."

"Ah! Leprechauns! Is that what I hear on the roof?"

Keely giggled wildly, jumped up and down, and clapped her hands. "No, that's my daddy!"

Taylor grinned, too warm and lazy to start the heavy work of sorting Maudie's things. She wiggled her toes against the patchwork quilt, stretched and yawned.

When she opened her eyes, Keely was studying her with interest. "I'm cold, too," she said uncertainly. "If you let me lay with you, I could tell you my daddy's stories. He tells good stories."

Taylor pushed aside what Quinn could do for leaving his daughter unattended. She settled for "Tell me about the leprechauns," Taylor responded, and lifted the quilt, an invitation for Keely.

Keely kicked off her shoes and scrambled into the bed. She lay on the delicate, red rosebud-spattered pillow and grinned at Taylor. "Well," she said, squirming closer to Taylor, "leprechauns make clothes, and they make shoes. They are tiny. This tiny." Keely placed her hands three inches apart.

"So small?" Taylor asked as one of the small hands found a length of her hair and stroked it. She caught the fragrance of baby powder, which reminded her of Quinn's scent the night before.

"My daddy said so," Keely stated with lofty authority. "If you can catch a leprechaun, he can lead you to a pot of gold." Her green eyes darkened with a thought before she pushed it away and continued, "My grandma says there are other kinds of fairies. 'Cause *her* grandma told her so when she was a little girl like me. Daddy uses my magic fairy dust—really it's baby powder, but I'm not a baby."

Taylor's mind flipped back to an uncertain teenage girl and the cold, rigid face of her grandmother. "How *dare* you!" Agatha Morely-Hart had hissed, pointing the tip of her cane at Taylor. "There has never been a bastard child in this family, and now you..."

Beside Taylor, Keely sighed tiredly. "You smell nice...and then, if you see a dust swirl, it could be a fairy dancing a jig. I know how to dance a jig.... They take baths every day...." Her voice drifted off, and she cuddled Queenie, who stared blankly up at Taylor.

Taylor eased a curl away from the girl's warm, soft cheek, stroking it with her fingertip. *Just for a few minutes,* she thought, allowing her eyes to close.

A few minutes of rest, and then she'd find Quinn and give him a piece of her mind.

"Quinn! Quinn Daniel!" At nine o'clock, Molly Donovan came rushing up Maudie's walkway, cupping her hands to call to her son.

Even from his perch on the roof, Quinn could see his mother's fear. "Up here!"

Molly clasped her hands in front of her chest, then scooped a corner of her apron up to dry her damp eyes. "Quinn, Keely isn't anywhere."

Her eyes shot fearfully to Ferguson Lake. "Oh, Quinn, do you think she..."

But he was already climbing down the ladder, taking the rungs two at a time and leaping the last six feet. His mother was trembling, and her face was pale with fear. Her fingers locked with his, and her eyes darted toward the lake. "Quinn, one minute she was sleeping on the couch, safe as could be, wrapped in the blanket you brought her in. I checked on her, then decided to start the beef in Guinness," she said hurriedly. The dish, meat cooked slowly in Irish beer, was a family favorite. "What with cutting the meat and onions and carrots, browning the meat and frying the onions, placing it in the pot, and then Laura Flynn called and wanted my toffee recipe—"

"Mother, what happened?" Quinn asked impatiently, interrupting her.

"Then, Quinn, Keely was gone! Just gone! I've searched and called, and the whole town is out hunting for her!" Her eyes widened, darting up to his. "Oh, dear Lord. Keely wouldn't have gone back to your millpond, would she?"

Quinn inhaled, tucking away the fear so that he could think clearly. He didn't want to look at Ferguson Lake or the millpond, so instead he looked into the garden nook where Keely liked to play, then to the spacious front porch.

He caught his mother's hand and nodded toward Queenie's doll carriage, by the slightly opened screen door. His mother's fingers dug into his arm. She feared the old house, with its steep basement stairs and laundry chute, and the kitchen knives.

Quinn moved through the house, silently, careful not to frighten Keely if she was near danger. The basement was dark, filled with Maudie's trunks and canned fruits and vegetables. Cobwebs lurked in the shadowy depths, not his daughter. Molly waited upstairs, shaking her head. Quinn surged up the stairs; he gently opened the first bedroom door, then Maudie's.

Molly was behind him, her eyes catching his grim scowl. She traced his gaze to the bed and the two females sleeping there.

Keely lay nestled against Taylor, the black cap of curls blending with Taylor's hair. The long curls spilled across the pillowcases and her breasts, covered by the old-fashioned high-collared nightgown. Keely's hand lay riding Taylor's chest, rising and falling slowly, gently.

Quinn's throat went dry, his heart beating in it.

"Oh, thank goodness she's all right." His mother sighed softly and added, "They're a pretty pair, aren't they?"

But Quinn was fighting the need to ease into that big bed and gather the woman and the child against him, keeping them safe. Instead, he cursed, a low damning sound that brought his mother's shocked blue eyes rising to his. "Quinn Daniel Donovan!" she admonished in a whisper. "I haven't heard that from you since I washed your mouth out with soap when you were eight."

She touched his arm, then murmured, "I'll call off the countryside, and you call off that fine temper you're brewing before they wake, boyo."

Quinn tried to breathe, to force air into his lungs. He tried to gather Keely in his arms to leave, but found he couldn't.

Instead, he knelt by the bed, taking his sleeping daughter's warm, slightly sticky hand in his and held it. His gaze followed Taylor's face, her fine, soaring brows. Her slicing, stormy eyes were closed, fringed by spiking lashes. The parting of her mouth was soft and inviting.

The beat in the hollow of her throat beckoned, and Quinn tensed, his stomach hurting. The steady lift of the nightgown's lace fluttered above the curve of a milky breast. Quinn forced himself to swallow, aware that his mouth had gone dry. Lodged in his body was a desire that would cost him more than a minute's pain.

Her eyes drifted open, fluttered, then slowly focused on him. The soft look slid away, replaced by steel.

"What are you doing, Donovan?" Taylor's hushed question slashed at him.

He refused to return the tone, refused to look away, shielding what was heating his body, racing through his heart.

Taylor caught the look, blinked, and widened her eyes. The blush crept slowly from her throat upward, and Quinn watched, fascinated, as her tongue moistened her lips.

Their eyes met and locked. Lightning and thunder raged in the quiet, lace-trimmed, lavender-scented room as Quinn trailed a fingertip along her jaw, then placed it on the racing pulse at the base of her throat. He stroked that smooth skin, felt the heat rising beneath it, the quick trembling that ran through Taylor—this woman he didn't want, *couldn't* want, in his life.

Taylor cleared her throat. Her lips moved, silently. Her voice, when it came, was husky, wary. "Would you please leave?" she whispered as Keely sighed and nestled closer.

The movement drew Taylor's nightgown aside, and Quinn's heart stopped. The curved side of her breast led to a dark shadow beneath the cloth. The shadow hardened into a nub, and the sight of that intimate feminine response drained every thought from him.

Taylor inhaled sharply, and Quinn turned slowly, to look into the eyes of the woman he wanted.

She frowned, her hand slowly pulling the quilt up to her throat. It pleased him that a shy blush ran beneath her skin, warming it. That she trembled with the emotions swirling between them.

A movement behind him brought him to his senses, and Molly winked at him. Her beaming expression said, *So, this is the one that tempted you off your shelf. How many shall we expect to the wedding, dear?*

Instead, Molly pushed down her smile enough to say, "Lovely. Lovely morning for coffee with a new neighbor. It will be ready in just a moment, dear. I'm Molly Donovan, Quinn's mother. You must be Maudie's heir."

Quinn rose to his feet, fighting the taut need riding him and wondering how he would deal with it. He needed to trim the soaring fear, the snare of this woman who brought his passions rising to the surface. "In a minute. First I want a word with Taylor about child-snatching—"

"Quinn! Mind your manners. You're standing in the lady's bedroom. Uninvited, might I add? Oh, and poor Keely, she looks exhausted."

Quinn decided not to discuss his daughter's lack of sleep. She had spent the night in his bed, worrying about getting a mother, worrying if she was the reason her mother had gone to heaven, worrying if Taylor would like her, and hoping to find a really good leprechaun in the morning. All Quinn's reassurances and attempts to distract her had been unsuccessful—Keely had fretted about her motherless state and about "Tay" being without children and within claiming distance.

Then Keely had sought out Taylor, and the sight of them together, warm and safe, had stopped his heart.

"He's a bit of a bully sometimes, my boy," Molly was saying, moving between Quinn and Taylor, gently shoving him out the door. "Go along now, boyo. Go about your business. It isn't fitting for an unmarried man to be in the bedroom of an unmarried woman."

A man yelled urgently, his footsteps pounding up the stairs, "Mother! Quinn! I was just getting grain at the feed store when I heard. Have you found Keely?"

"Shush!" Molly ordered, her eyes lifting to the newcomer, a man older and broader than Quinn, his face fierce with concern. "My son, Cadell Michael. He farms his father's land now." Shorter than her sons by over a foot, Molly lifted a hand to swat at her older son's battered, dusty western hat. She missed by several inches when he lifted his head. Dressed in a worn western shirt, jeans and boots, he eased slightly into the doorway, the tension draining from him. He looked at Keely, who remained sleeping, then at the woman at her side. His black eyes, set in a thick frame of lashes like Quinn's, slid down Taylor's body beneath the quilt, then back up to her face. Taylor sensed a friendly, secure warmth, unlike Quinn's untamed challenges and heat.

"I'm coming in from the ranch more often. Things are looking up," the older man said in a deep, melodic voice. "The name is Cade, ma'am."

Quinn inhaled sharply, and Molly ordered, "Cadell, take off your hat in the presence of a lady. This is Taylor Hart. Maudie was her great-aunt."

Keely sighed and snuggled her cheek against Taylor's chest. "My mommy..." she sighed, at ease with the hushed adults talking in the room.

Taylor cuddled the girl closer, because the soft drape of the child's body was precious, and because she needed whatever protection she could find at hand against the stormy, sensual vibrations coming from Quinn.

Cade kissed his fingertip and placed it on Keely's round cheek, "Thank God she's safe."

"Nice meeting you, Cade," Taylor murmured, meaning it. There was a solemn, sturdy look to Cade. Then he glanced at Quinn's dark scowl and turned to wink at her like a conspirator. She liked him instantly.

"Ma'am." The older man dutifully removed his hat; the light in the room caught on the touch of gray shot through his dark wavy hair and the harsh, angular features resembling Quinn's. His hard mouth softened, and he turned slowly to Quinn and lifted his brows at his brother's dark scowl. "Well, well... So Keely has finally caught her leprechaun and got her wish—"

Quinn inhaled sharply and moved toward his brother.

Molly edged between her tall sons, placing a restraining hand on each broad chest, as though they were still boys. "Hush, now, Cadell. Stop tormenting poor Quinn. He's had enough of a fright for one day. We all have."

"If you're done looking, Cadell, you can leave," Quinn stated, moving impatiently, his body tense.

"Ah... *Cadell*, is it? You must be mad enough to chew nails to use that name with me. You're standing here, too, aren't you, boyo?" Cade returned teasingly. "Besides that, the lady goes easy on the eyes. Pretty as a picture, lying there with your daughter.... Does things to a man," he mused slowly, the lines around his eyes deepening.

Molly jerked a quick glance up to Quinn's rigid face. She beamed, looking at Taylor's slender left hand. "Are you married, dear?"

For a heartbeat, uncertainty flitted through Taylor's still-drowsy eyes as they jerked from Molly's kind, expectant smile to Quinn's dark scowl. "Well, I... No... No, I'm not."

Quinn shared a look with his mother, his eyes narrowing menacingly before Cade lifted a thick eyebrow and Molly's beaming smile grew. "Shoo now, Quinn. Go along and do whatever Maudie wanted. Cadell, there's fresh bread and a roast cooked for you to take back to the ranch. There were cookies and milk waiting for you until Quinn's scamp of a daughter raided them. I want to talk with Maudie's niece, Taylor. What a wonderful name," she said, continuing to nudge her tall sons from the room.

Quinn shot Taylor a warning look over his shoulder. She tossed it back at him, and then dimples flirted in her cheeks and she murmured smugly, "Yes. Why don't you just...go away?"

He stopped in midstep, jerked his frown to Cade, who smothered a low chuckle, then back to Taylor. "Easy now, boyo," Cade murmured. "This one can hold her own."

"'He promised Maudie that the house would be painted for me...and Quinn always keeps his promises,'" Taylor repeated Molly's tidbit darkly, tracking the footsteps on the roof. "A tiny leprechaun he isn't."

At midmorning, she sat at Maudie's table, sipping the last of the coffee she had made to share earlier with Molly. Taylor had learned that Briana, the baby of the family, could twist her older brothers around her little finger. And that where Cade's emotions were deep and sheltered, Quinn and Bria followed their hearts.

Keely had slipped into Taylor's lap from her grandmother's and shared the bowl of Maudie's peaches. The little girl's eyes were hopeful and adoring as she cuddled close, clearly entranced by Taylor. In return, Taylor admitted ruefully, she was enchanted by the little girl, who hungered for a mother. "My mommy is in heaven," she had murmured wistfully, laying her head against Taylor's chest.

The warmth of Molly's smile stilled, hovered and dropped away, too quickly.

When the house was quiet, Taylor settled down to the task in front of her. After reading a few letters from Maudie's many dear friends, Taylor decided against having her assistant do a mass mailing. Taking stationery sprayed with violet designs, she wrote the necessary notes, as gently as possible. As an afterthought, she added her business address, in case Maudie's friends needed—needed what? Comforting? Reassurance?

Then, to soften words that seemed inadequate, she placed a sprig of Maudie's dried herbs in each small envelope. They crushed easily, just as easily as lives. Or a child's heart.

In her lifetime, Taylor had had little experience dealing with the gentler issues. Maudie's friends' letters, however, were filled with caring tidbits and endearments about their families.

Taylor's eyes skimmed Maudie's beloved garden, picturing the elderly woman caring for the flowers and herbs. A scarlet bolt soared from the trees to Maudie's empty bird feeder, and suddenly a red cardinal tilted his head at the kitchen window, wanting his breakfast. Taylor jotted a note to find a caretaker, someone to care for the gardens and fill the bird feeders until the property was sold. Another, smaller iridescent bullet shot by Maudie's curtain window, and a tiny hummingbird hovered in front of an empty feeder designed especially for him. Taylor found herself smiling. "I'm working on it. Drop in at teatime."

Later, with the stack of notes addressed beside her, she frowned and wondered when she had ever sent personal notes. She flipped open her business notebook and jotted down a reminder to shop for intimate stationery.

The old house snuggled around her, filled with scents and color. Sunlight tangled in the lemony lace at the window, then splashed onto the yellow squares of linoleum. Taylor shook her head. The house was as enticing as the freshly baked bread that Molly had sent by way of Travis Donovan, a man in his early twenties.

Taylor rarely stayed in one place very long. Her personal belongings were few, able to be packed and unpacked eas-

ily. Her life was deliberately uncluttered, a contrast to
Maudie, whose house and beautiful handcrafted furniture
seemed to reflect years of friendships.

Taylor slashed open the usual business mail, setting aside
the large, crisp business envelopes with the Randolph Developers markings. She stood and stretched, then wandered out to the back porch. Late-May sunlight danced in
the oaks and on the walkway leading toward the lake. Flat
brown native rocks warmed the soles of her feet. The
chamomile growing between the rocks released a delicious,
tangy-sweet scent. Taylor's eyes skimmed the rolling hills
and thick forests dressed in different shades of green.

Randolph Developers's generous offer portrayed an ex-
pansive plan for an elite resort and condominiums set in the
hills near Blarney. According to the developers Blarney Flats
would profit from employment and tourism.

The breeze caught in the water and a swirl of ripples went
scooting across the small, calm lake, taking Taylor's
thoughts with it. The walkway led closer to the water,
drawing her. Taylor followed it, enchanted by a clearing in
which sat a small bench overlooking the lake. A wooden
ramp led into the lake and, tied to it, a fishing boat bobbed
gently in the water.

Instinct told her another person shared the sunlight dap-
pling the pathway. Or was it the way the hair lifted on the
nape of her neck, the way heat flowed down her backside?
"Quinn," she stated flatly, catching the scent of paint,
wood, sun and man and crossing her arms protectively in
front of her.

"Thank you," he murmured stiffly, as she turned slowly.
Quinn, dressed in worn joggers and jeans marked by paint
and tantalizing holes, held a spray of woodland flowers and
aromatic herbs.

Taylor tried to take her eyes from an expanse of darkly
tanned skin, from the crisp black hair covering his chest and
glistening in the sun. An erotic stripe of pink paint crossed
the dark width like a soaring arrow to the heart. Quinn's
corded shoulders gleamed in the dappled sunlight, and his

untamed hair lifted with the breeze from the lake. Another pink slash flowed along his cheek as though it had been impatiently wiped away. A drop caught in the rough stubble covering his jaw, and a trail of pink dots crossed a gleaming black brow.

A delicate, buttery petal escaped the bouquet and tumbled down to nestle in the hair covering Quinn's chest.

Rogue. Barbarian. Do-little, non-upwardly mobile backwoods…hunk…dish… She tried to tear her eyes away, and couldn't. In another moment, she'd be drooling.

Taylor wondered when she had last drooled over a man and then decided that until this time—now, here with Quinn Donovan—there hadn't been cause.

The scent of the flowers and herbs curled between them. Quinn's unusual dark emerald eyes flowed down the long sleeves of her cream knit shirt to the loose brown slacks catching the wind. Touched by his dark look, Taylor's toes tingled before his gaze slowly began to rise.

Her upper thighs melted and tingled. The pit of her stomach dropped lower and heated.

His gaze caressed her crossed arms, and Taylor belatedly realized that the movement had served to lift her breasts higher. She cleared her throat, and the hard, clipped tone she'd intended slid into a breathless, husky whisper. "Why are you thanking me?"

Swallowing to moisten her dry throat, Taylor found her upper arms hurting because her nails were digging into them.

She resented that loss of control, the emotional tugs warring inside her. Her breath sucked in as he shifted and the worn jeans sagged lower on his hips. She jerked her eyes up to his and found them soft, richly tinted, like a summer meadow. A reckless need to clutch Quinn's broad, gleaming shoulders and take what she wanted surged through her. What exactly did she want? she wondered.

She sensed that taking a kiss from Quinn would be no simple matter. For one thing, he loomed over her as few men did.

For another, she sensed that beneath that mouth-watering exterior there lurked a darkness he hid well; Taylor doubted that anyone could take anything from him that he didn't allow.

He held out the bouquet, lacy bits of fuchsia and blue nestled among stalks of scented herbs. They quivered—or was it her heart? Yet the hard, capable hand dashed with pink paint held them securely. She sensed that Quinn would hold everything precious to him just as safely. For once Taylor doubted her ability to keep herself free of entanglements. Quinn Donovan was surely an enticement, his head tilted intimately down at her. "For keeping Keely safe."

She inhaled sharply. If the garden-fresh flowers were a seduction enticing her senses, the man was a hunger.

Caught by her smoky gaze, Quinn had wanted to—wanted to what? He'd seen her leave the house, this willowy, fiercely independent woman. Her loose designer slacks had caught the breeze, rippling against long legs. She'd bound her hair in an unforgiving knot, but the breeze had tugged free tendrils that danced around her face and the long line of her neck.

Scents, cool, exotic and womanly, hovered with the flowery ones, beckoning to him. Quinn's gaze traced the striking, aristocratic cheekbones, the wide dark blue eyes, the fine nose, and her mouth—trembling, slightly parted and vulnerable—which wiped his thoughts away as he handed her the flowers.

She took them solemnly, though a quick glance down at the blooms and a drift of her fingers across them told him she was pleased. Then a tiny dimple tugged in her cheek before it stilled.

Her genuine pleasure surprised him. This woman must have had mountains of florists' flowers.

The memory of her lying with his child, the soft drowsiness lurking in her dark blue eyes, slammed into Quinn again. The lacy, old-fashioned collar that had caressed her breast would haunt him forever. He'd wondered how she would look after lovemaking. How she would look after *his* lovemaking, he corrected fiercely.

She caught the dark look, and her head came up, her eyes meeting his. Because she pleased him, Quinn took a step closer, and she shivered. He chuckled, sliding a finger along her cool cheek to flick a shimmering tendril.

Taylor moved aside and her cool scents beckoned him. "If you sell Ferguson Lake, Hart, will the buyers care for the monster?" he found himself asking.

Her dark blue eyes flicked at him warily. "The what?"

Quinn fought a moment, then gave in to his first impulse. "The baby Loch Ness. Baby has only been around for fifty years. His mother was seventy-five when she was last seen some decades ago."

"Impossible." Yet Taylor turned to the lake, scanning the glassy blue surface and nuzzling the flowers thoughtfully.

Quinn inhaled the alluring, cool scents of Taylor. He studied the proud lift of her head, the slender fingers shading her view of the lake. "Ferguson's curse. A four-thousand-pound, forty-foot monster roaming the depths of the lake, snatching unbelievers from the shore and their boats. Ferguson—Laird Ferguson—is buried in the midst of the Irish immigrants he cursed, a Scotsman's plaid carved on his stone. So the Irish planted shamrocks—or rather lawn clover—over his grave."

Quinn noted the quick, whimsical jerk of her mouth and the indentation of a beguiling dimple before it stilled.

"You're full of blarney, Donovan," she stated easily, turning to him.

The humor lurking in her eyes caught him, twisted around his heart and snared him deeper. "Maybe. But the fish—a species of small shad that the monster is said to protect—do exist and are unique to the lake. Biologists say they're an endangered species, and that the slightest shift of the lake's ecological balance could lose them for eternity."

The laughter in her eyes died as she scanned the lake, heavily bordered by trees. "I'll check into it. There's a nice offer for the property...an exclusive condominium and golf course. Because Maudie liked the community so much, the proceeds would go to Blarney."

How could he blame Keely for her fascination, when his stirred so wildly? he thought as Taylor moved, impatient to be away from him.

Hadn't he learned his lesson the first time when Nancy snared him into her net?

"You'll be gone soon enough," he murmured, fighting needs he didn't want to recognize. The *squeak-squeak* of Keely's tricycle stopped, then began again as she made her rounds past Maudie's house, and Donovan thought of this woman and his daughter nestled together in the big brass bed. To cover the trail of his thoughts, he lashed at her. "Make certain that when you go you don't hurt my daughter."

She jerked back from him, crossing her arms. "I'm aware of the dangers of a child's attachment to a passing stranger. I wouldn't want Keely hurt, either. I'll keep my distance."

He struck out at her, angered by his reactions to her. "So you keep your relationships neat. Do you monitor them, like so much profit and loss? What do you do, count them at night, weigh each one and pack them away so they can't touch you? So you prefer to travel light.... How will you survive without daily conferences, your staff?"

She settled back then, her head tilting to one side, challenging him. "I manage, Donovan."

"You'll be gone soon enough," he repeated softly, enchanted by the flush heating Taylor's milky skin. To taunt her further, he tucked a fuchsia flower in the tightly drawn hair at her temple. Quinn's fingertip stroked her hair once before her head jerked back. "And what will you leave in your wake?"

She shifted restlessly, easing away from him. "I know the town cared for Maudie, and she loved them. I'll do the best job I can. I've always taken care of my responsibilities."

"And who takes care of you?" Not allowing her the space she wanted, he slid a finger along that long, soft throat.

She shivered. "You're pushing, and trust me, I don't like being forced into corners. I've been taking care of myself for years, Donovan. If you think buttering me up will sway my judgment, you're mistaken. Move out of my way."

Because she looked so fierce, so alone, Quinn dropped the thought of how he'd like to butter her from toes to mouth. He found himself bending, nearing her wide smoky blue eyes to brush her lips lightly with his.

She smiled at Quinn, a probing, speculative look that he
returned easily enough. "Perhaps it would help us to talk for
a while," Antiqua remarked. "I don't know if I will be any
help to you, but perhaps it's the least of it."

Before she could reject it, as he knew she just might,
Antiqua rose and strolled away into the trees to collect the
basket. Closing her eyes, as if she were too weary to care,
Taylor resisted the impulse to call him back.

Four

"**H**ow dare you!" Taylor snapped furiously. She stepped
back, and a flat rock shifted with her weight, sending her off
balance. Surprise and alarm skipped over her face. Quinn
cursed, reached to snare her hand and missed. Taylor fell
backward into a thick bramble of thorny blackberries.

"Hold still," he ordered sharply, bending to pluck her
free before she settled fully.

"Don't tell me what to do, you..." she shot back as he
swept her against his chest. "Put me down, you big jerk."

Quinn carried her to the picnic table. "Stop throwing a
hissy fit, Hart, before I toss you back."

"Let me down, Donovan," Taylor ordered from between her teeth, with enough ice in her voice to freeze the
flowers she had gripped throughout her fall. He noted she
kept them close, protecting them as best she could.

He had the satisfaction of seeing her white with rage, the
willowy body humming with it. He gathered her closer,
damning the instinct to protect her. He hefted her gently and

frowned when she winced. "Lady, your class A backside is decorated with Maudie's best blackberry thorns."

"'Class A'? How dare you. How dare you!" she snapped again. The storms in her dark blue eyes lashed out at him.

Quinn wasn't spending time on an anatomy debate. He'd caught her before her weight landed fully in the briars; the thorns should be lodged at the surface of her clothing. He glanced at the tiny scratches on her wrist. "You can't walk without driving them deeper. You can't sit, either."

Taylor inhaled, and her hair began to slide free. She pushed at it, caught his eyes trailing down to her thrusting breasts, then crossed her arms in front of her. "Well?"

Quinn had to grin. She frowned darkly. "Well?" she prompted, this time impatiently. "You live here. What's the protocol? And by the way, what's a 'hissy fit'?" she demanded.

He allowed his grin to widen, though his heart raced at the thought of her fine, milky flesh scratched by briars. "It's a temper fit that hisses. Quinn Donovan at your service, Hart. There's a procedure that will stop matters from worsening."

"And that is?" she demanded flatly.

"Since I doubt that I can carry you all the way to the house, I'll lay you down just as gently as possible on this picnic table. We take off your drawers, with most of the thorns, and from there it's a matter of pick and pluck."

"Pick and pluck? Lay me down on the picnic table?" she repeated blankly, scanning the redwood surface.

"On your stomach, Hart. Your backside needs attention."

Her fist grabbed his shirt, jerking it tight. "You caused this, Donovan. Put me down."

"Can't. The thorns will go deeper in your feet." Quinn pushed away the horrible sight of Taylor falling into the brambles again.

"Now," she ordered tightly, holding herself stiffly away from his chest. To do so, she placed one hand on him, and Quinn felt the shudder of pain rippling through her. While he waited, she lifted her palm and frowned at the thorns she had driven deeper. Taylor glanced at his chest, her frown deepening as she plucked a thorn from her finger. "They're on you, too."

He hadn't noticed the trickle of blood from the thorns that had pricked his arms as he scooped her free. He'd thought only of the need to keep her safe. "It's best done quickly," he said as her eyes flowed across him, touching, seeking, widening. When her gaze lingered at his mouth, Quinn sucked in his breath. "Easy," he said, more to calm his thundering heart than to reassure her.

Taylor shuddered, and a wild tumble of hair came down. "I am not letting you..." She hesitated, her expression wary. "I'm not about to let you touch me."

He hefted her gently, testing the grimace of pain flitting across her face. "You're a bully, Donovan. One to take advantage of opportunities. You could lay me down, then go for help," she pointed out warily.

"I could," he agreed easily. He had no intention of leaving her alone. Taylor was just stubborn enough to try to walk, and the thorns would sink deeper with the slightest pressure. "Gossip runs free in Blarney. I'm no more anxious to be caught in it than you. With us both in brambles, the first implication would be that we had a roll in the bushes. I have a reputation to uphold. Can't have people snickering about my charm. I wouldn't deny that you'd thrown yourself at me, of course."

She snorted delicately. "Charm? There's a word for it. Keely has charm. You're a bully. You've got the upper hand, and you're using it. For now." Then she added, as an afterthought, "The day I throw myself at you..."

He shrugged. "Well, then, it's easy to see how afraid you are of me. In a minute you'll gasp and faint away from fright."

"Me gasp and faint? The day I'm afraid of an oversize jerk like you..."

While Quinn waited, entranced by the expressions flowing across her face, she weighed the matter for a full second, then said warily, "I don't want gossip—this incident to reflect badly upon Aunt Maudie. I won't have people say— I suppose you'd be no different from a masseuse, if you took that clinical attitude."

"On my honor," Quinn pledged, meaning it.

She sighed—a resigned release of air held too long. "You seem to have the upper hand at the moment. Pluck away, Donovan."

While helping Taylor ease her shirt and slacks away, Quinn debated the foolishness of promising anything. The light camisole and cotton briefs had only a few thorns, most of them over her bottom. Lying on her stomach, she watched him warily over her shoulder as he worked his way down her back. "This wouldn't have happened—" She inhaled sharply as he plucked a thorn free from her bottom. She rubbed the wound briskly, inhaled, then continued. "If you hadn't been making a move."

Quinn swept his hand lightly over her long back, watching the pale skin ripple beneath his hand. The drape of Taylor's expensive clothing had shielded the slender curves, the gently rounded hips. "When I choose to 'make a move,' women usually acknowledge it," he returned flatly, truthfully.

He neglected to add that his moves had all been before his marriage and not a one after his divorce. He worked quickly, wiping away the fine sweat on his brow with the back of his hand. He wrapped his fingers around a slender ankle and jerked it higher, plucking thorns quickly.

Soft flesh beneath practical pale blue briefs jiggled just once as she shifted. Unable to force his eyes away from the soft, cotton-covered flesh, Quinn waited for his heartbeat to start again. Then he found his hand squeezing her upper thigh possessively before he forced it away.

Hell. He would rather tangle with Ferguson's monster in a tornado than face his sharpening desire for this woman. He wiped his sweaty cheek with his upper arm and jerked her other foot up for his inspection.

Slender and well shaped, Taylor's toes wiggled against his stomach. He watched, air caught in his lungs, as they lingered, twitching in the hair around his navel. The flexing of her arches locked him in place. A thin leash kept him from bending his mouth to kiss the tender white curve.

Stunned by the desire lurching through him, Quinn eased her toes aside.

"I don't want a word of this slipping out, Donovan. One word and I'll drive you into the ground."

He shrugged aside the threat, but could not ignore the rising heat knotting his stomach. "Done," he muttered, striding to the water faucet nearby. "With the exception of my mother. She'll come over to tend those scratches. In the meantime, take a bath with baking soda to take out the sting."

"I don't need—"

"Her or me," he ordered flatly, pushing away thoughts of Taylor's long, pale body beneath his on the big brass bed. "Which is it?"

"Take a note, Donovan," she said between her teeth. "I don't like being forced into corners." Then, very properly: "If Molly can fit it into her schedule, I would appreciate the time."

He nodded. Bending his head beneath the cold water served to ease his tension. He lifted his gaze to find Taylor watching him curiously. Her long, pale elegant body gleamed in the shadows, sharpening his desire. Hunger stalked Taylor's stormy eyes and the soft part of her lips before she looked away.

"Donovan has nerve," Taylor muttered late that afternoon as she jerked away the dustcovers from Maudie's furniture. After her bath and Molly's delicate removal of the remaining thorns and disinfecting of the small scratches, Taylor had spent the afternoon accepting casseroles and baked goods from the lovely elderly people along Hummingbird Lane. Each dish was delicious, and she'd sampled them all. She sampled them again when she thought of

ying under the flow of Donovan's strong, rough, callused
hands. He liked having her under his thumb, and she'd never
liked bullies—even bullies with gentle hands.

She learned from the residents of Hummingbird Lane that
they didn't share her dark view of him. Quinn took care of
their fix-up needs. He'd recently installed a walkway for
Mazie Waters's wheelchair and widened her old house's
doorways. Clearly Donovan was the darling of the town,
second only to his daughter, who rode her tricycle daily
along the street, visiting at each house.

Last week, Keely had a really good sale on baby mice
found in her grandmother's back shed. In a few weeks,
she'd be delivering fresh "monster" tomatoes from Molly
and James Donovan's massive garden.

Taylor's office had called about a series of calamities, and
she'd postponed an important conference call. She worried
about the details of a special project—in a matter of weeks,
the terms for the takeover of a small electronic firm would
be final, but the deal needed her touch as a negotiator.

Then there was Quinn. disturbing her thoughts when she
wanted to concentrate on business.

"Swaggering jerk." She closed her lids, and behind them
strolled a vision of Donovan, raw and untamed, lifting his
head from the faucet. Water had streamed down his wet
hair, droplets bounced in the sunlight, falling to his shoulders and streaming down his chest as he shook his head. He
had rinsed his arms quickly, a magnificent beast in the
shadows, a blend of corded muscles, dark skin and rippling
flat stomach.

His jeans had sagged low on his hips, baring a pale strip
of flesh. An intriguing wedge of dark hair had flowed across
his chest and narrowed as it flowed into his jeans. Her
mouth had dried, and her eyes had locked to the long, hard
line of his body, which was as delectable as raspberry jam
and melting butter on freshly baked bread.

He'd caught her look and sauntered toward her, water
streaming from his hair, droplets gleaming in the dark hair
covering his chest. The worn jeans had tightened over his

arousal, and the notion that he wanted her had caught Taylor broadside, stunning her. Her body had tingled, her thighs softening as she stared helplessly. A dangerous man set on his course, Quinn had looked deeply into her eyes, then raised her palms to his mouth, his lips easing the small lacerations.

At the time, Quinn might have been playing seduction games, but she hadn't been. Little had kept her from grabbing those broad shoulders and jerking him against her. She'd wanted to lay him down on the picnic table and feast upon him.

Taylor blinked. She had led a controlled, orderly life. Until Quinn.

She hated her weakness, and she hated Donovan for wearing his masculinity so casually, so arrogantly. In the space of two days, he'd turned her comfortable world inside out. Quinn left no room for her safe, cool margin of emotional distance. She hadn't drooled after a man in her lifetime. Nor had a man broadsided her with so many emotions. Quinn couldn't possibly know that she had a weakness for fables and folklore. "Baby Loch Ness monster. I wonder how many women have fallen for that one."

Then that whimsical, sweet kiss before he'd swaggered away, leaving her stomach in knots and her mouth dry.

And aching.

It had been a full minute before she trusted herself to stand, her knees almost buckling beneath her.

She slammed a dust sheet against a delicate rocking chair. It rocked back and forth, creaking. The flowers shivered in the breeze flowing through the open window, and Taylor closed her eyes, willing the picture of Quinn—untamed and exciting—away forever.

A quick call to a biologist friend proved Donovan was correct about the species of shad and the delicate balance of the lake's ecological system. The biologist was familiar with the species of shad. He stated that any manipulation of the small lake—the runoff of dirt caused by bulldozers—would upset the delicate fish. Rainfall could carry pesticides comnonly used in landscaping into the lake and could destroy the natural ecological balance.

The biologist stated that the lake had been studied and was unspoiled and unique. He offered his assistance and noted stiffly that several developers had first asked his opinion, then hired a private research staff.

Keely's tricycle went creak-creaking by slowly. Taylor watched the little girl as she peered longingly at the old house, trying to see past the lace curtains. Then, slowly, she tucked Queenie against her with one arm, and the tricycle began moving up the street, pulling a small red wagon.

The telephone rang a few moments later, and Ophelia Davenport, Maudie's neighbor, said, "Keely is at my place.... I know you're only here for a few days, but we'd appreciate you calling ahead when Keely makes her rounds on clear days. That way we know she's safe. Dear, sweet child. When she's ready to leave my house, I call Sara Dooley and she calls Rosie Whitehouse and so forth. Then, when Keely goes back to town... I used to call Maudie...."

There was a pause and a sniff. "Well, dear, I'll call when Keely comes back. If you could call Quinn, that would be helpful. She has five minutes to make the distance to the millhouse, and he watches her all the way."

Taylor hesitated, inhaled, then agreed. Ophelia chatted a while about a rose blight that had worried Maudie, then murmured, "We think Keely is so precious, and Quinn is a darling. He helps all of us. Our children and grandchildren all live away. Such a dear boy. By the way, Keely is hunting desperately for a leprechaun to make her wish for a mother come true. And she's got her sights set on you.... I'm so glad Quinn is keeping up the pink trim on Maudie's house. She loved pink and blue. I've been thinking about asking him for yellow. My Alfred, the dear old thing, has made Quinn more of his fishing lures. Quinn repaired the leak in Alfred's boat. Come over when you can, dear. I used to have tea with Maudie every afternoon about this time."

Taylor scanned the parlor. The old furniture gleamed beneath a thin layer of dust. A board creaked, and through the open window flowed a gentle breeze laden with the lime scent of geraniums, Maudie's favorite. Then there was the fragrance of thyme and the scarlet roses climbing the freshly painted trellis.

Maudie's clothing, neatly folded and packed in boxes and suitcases, was stacked in a corner. An open box stood in the center of the room, waiting. Taylor closed her eyes, fighting the welling of emotion that filled her throat and dampened her eyes.

She dashed the back of her hand across her lids, rubbing the moisture away on her slacks. A teardrop fell to her cheek, then another, and Taylor found herself unraveling slowly, her sobs blending with years of loneliness and echoing through the sunlit parlor....

"A bastard with the Hart name? Never!" Agatha Morely-Hart's shriek sliced into Taylor. "An affair with a married man? How dare you think that I'd believe for a moment that Ernest Lang committed adultery? Rape?" Her shriek ricocheted through time. "Rape? You dallied in some dirty little place with a boy, Taylor. Now that the truth is out, and you've been caught, you're trying to save face. You've always been a rebel, and your lies could bring down two of the most prominent families in this town."

The lacy curtains fluttered with whispers, accusations, and Taylor huddled in a shadowy corner. While her mother had whimpered, the flat of her father's hand still burned on Taylor's cheek. *"Get rid of it,"* he'd ordered, his face florid with rage.

Later, a second slap from Ernest Lang brought the taste of blood, a taste she'd never forgotten.

Now, in the distance, Taylor heard a familiar *squeak-squeak* and a shudder ran through her. Ophelia telephoned then, and Taylor assured her she would call Quinn. She inhaled and tore herself from the past, taking another deep breath to steady her nerves. She eased aside the lace curtain to see Keely on her tricycle, Queenie clutched close against her. The little girl stared at the house as she passed, the *squeak-squeak*s slowing, and the pain in Taylor's heart eased a bit.

Even though she was desperately tired, she'd discovered a bit of peace in the old house, with its sounds and Maudie's beloved treasures. It frightened yet beckoned, tangling her in its serenity and timelessness, while children played nearby.

In their backyard, Ophelia called to Alfred, who bent to pluck a rose and hold it out to her. The colorful gingerbread trim on the turn-of-the-century houses caught the sunlight.

Taylor swallowed, dashing away the tears. In the end, she'd faced her family and their alliances, a powerful, successful woman, just as controlled as they were. Ernest had made the mistake of smirking, just once. Years later, she had taken his company apart, bit by bit, then walked away.

She remembered Quinn's unquestioned love for Keely and shuddered. She dialed his number, and he picked up the call instantly. The buzz of a machine slowed and stopped, and then she heard a rough, absent "Quinn."

"Keely's on her way home."

The woman's voice, low and soft and laden with tears, caught Quinn; his hand flattened on the smooth oak of the antique dry sink. His gut clenched instantly, and he carefully set aside the small hand drill.

He looked outside to see Keely pedaling her tricycle home, her curls dancing in the afternoon light. From her expression, he knew she couldn't wait to tell her news. "Hart?" he asked cautiously, remembering her stunned expression when he'd kissed her earlier. "Are you all right?"

There was the hiss of indrawn breath, a pause, and then a flat "Get off my case, Donovan. I've been taking care of myself for a long time."

The sound of tears lacing Taylor's voice a moment before held him still, his hand on the receiver, even after the line went dead. That low, uneven husky tone swirled around him long after Keely slept.

At midnight, Quinn slammed the flat of his hand on the smoothly sanded surface of an antique cherry buffet.

He stroked the curved front drawers. He should know better; he'd barely survived a woman just like Hart, and now here he was, asking for a second helping.

Quinn inhaled, pressed his lips together and jerked his hand from the smooth wood.

He pushed away the memory of the soft, startled clinging of her lips beneath his, the enticing scents, cool and beckoning, with a curl of the exotic beneath them.

Taylor would take her profits from the sale of Maudie's property and fly away. He had to protect Keely.

Or was it himself?

"Now there goes a woman for you, Donovan," Lyle Flynn murmured the next morning. He hefted the big sack of corn Quinn had ground coarsely for chicken feed into the back of his truck. He turned to wink at Quinn, who couldn't take his eyes from Taylor as she ran down the hill toward Blarney. Since the main and only street was one block from the millhouse, he could see her easily.

At six in the morning, the mists were shifting on the mill-pond, burning away in the dawn and the shadows of the surrounding hills. Taylor's long, bare legs moved in an easy stride, and her T-shirt clung to her breasts as she sailed down the slight hill from Maudie's. Tied into a ponytail, her black mane caught the sunlight, sailing like a gleaming flag. "She called our cousin, Sheriff Moriarity, for directions to the cemetery. She wants to visit Maudie. I believe I'd have other uses for the woman's morning energy if I were single and a fine specimen like that was running free," Lyle said, winking at Quinn again.

Quinn turned slowly to him, used to friendly nudging from his cousins. The sight of Taylor's endless legs hadn't soothed his nerves after a night spent dreaming about them. "I suppose your mouth will keep running whether anyone's listening or not."

Lyle grinned, gold glinting on a front tooth. "Orson says your black mood is due to the Hart woman. Moriarity told him. The story came from Moriarity's sister, Mary Faye, who watched the two of you dance. Said no one had ever seen you get so worked up. Said you held her tight against you and steamed. Said your ears got pointy."

He stroked his chin thoughtfully. "Makes a body wonder now, don't it? Here you are, minding your own business, pushing down your manly needs and denying the ladies hereabouts...then wham! You get all worked up over a lean, lanky, cool piece of all-business woman. According to Mary Faye, Maudie's niece didn't act all that excited about you. Bets are on the woman . . . just how long she'll take to drag you from your hole. Those who have faith in your charm say you can make her dance to your tune."

"Would you like to step behind the building, Lyle?" Quinn invited lightly. "That is, if you can stop talking long enough to roll up your tongue from the floor and put it in your mouth."

Lyle grinned wider. He jerked down his worn western hat, the straw rolled at the brim by his hand. "The Donovans have always been too touchy, boyo," he said. "Comes from the blend of Irish, Osage Native American and Russian gypsy blood."

"If you're wanting a taste of what comes from the blend of Irish, Russian and Osage blood, keep talking," Quinn warned lightly as Taylor sailed past the pub. The morning coffee crew filed out to the sidewalk, sipping from their mugs and timing Taylor with their watches. When she returned, long legs flying, her shirt pasted with sweat, they stepped onto the cobblestones and watched her pass. From the heated exchange that followed, the glances at the watches and the coins changing hands, Quinn knew the betting was on. Blarney's residents had been stirred from their routines. They were famous for friendly betting. Taylor's visit would take the pressure from the customary friendly Donovan-versus-Flynn disputes.

"She's flat as a boy," Lyle noted clinically. Quinn tightened his lips, looking closer. Unless he missed his guess, Taylor had bound her breasts.

That tantalizing thought started him sweating.

Interested in the flying ripple of Taylor's shorts, the smooth curve of her bottom and her long, gently muscled legs, Quinn didn't notice the crowd until he turned.

Fingers pointed toward him; John Seemore scribbled bets in his well-worn black book. Recognizing the scenario, Quinn's eyes narrowed.

"I'd better get over there," Lyle stated cheerfully. "I want in on the betting. From the looks of that fine sweat you're wearing, Donovan, my money is on the woman."

Quinn took a deep breath as Taylor surged up the hill. She'd be gone soon, and then he could finish the pink gingerbread trim. With luck, whoever purchased Maudie's land would listen to reason about Ferguson Lake. Then everything would settle down.

Maybe.

By evening, Quinn had heard about "the Hart woman" no fewer than seventy times. She'd parked her fancy rented car in front of the grocery store and purchased fresh vegetables. Nancy O'Reilly and Monique Layton had decided that the Hart woman was a "bean-sprouter"—the local name for a health-food addict. Her purchase—one sack, according to Mac, the grocer—had ran to pasta and fresh fruits and vegetables. The mailman had been instructed to deposit her mail in the box at Maudie's front door. The locals had timed her run at dusk at a fraction of a second slower than her morning run. Moriarity had carefully patrolled the exact distance from Maudie's house to the historic statue of Saint Patrick in the old city park, doubled it and pronounced that the Hart woman could run 6.4 miles without breathing hard.

That night, Keely snuggled in her father's arms and listened to her favorite dragon and fairy stories, just slightly impatient. When the good purple dragon singed the bottoms of the evil trolls and the princess and prince soared away on a feather, Keely kissed him. Wide meadow green eyes came close to his, and Keely stroked his evening stubble with her small hand.

"Daddy, Tay said I have to ask you if I can come to her house."

Quinn kissed Keely's nose, rubbing it with his. "Tay?" he asked, knowing the answer.

"Tay," Keely repeated firmly. "She lives in Maudie's house now. She said it was okay if I call her Tay, Daddy," his daughter said primly. She looked away. "I...uh... dropped Queenie's dress on the sidewalk in front of her house, and..."

While rocking Keely, Quinn mentally translated her lengthy, detailed story. Keely's "Tay" had just happened to be outside the house, looking up at the unfinished pink trim. Keely, a genius at invitations, had noted that Tay looked sad and her eyes held tears. His daughter was certain that visits from Queenie and herself could cheer Tay immensely...if it was okay with her daddy.

The story went on, saturated with his daughter's fascination with Taylor. Keely yawned, snuggling against him. "Tay is lonesome, Daddy," she whispered at last. "I kissed her tears, like you do mine, and told her that Maudie's fairies would take care of her. Tomorrow Grandma said she'd help me look for a really good leprechaun."

While Keely had her problems, Quinn had his. When he finally slept, he awoke dripping with sweat and fully aroused. Without hesitating, he ripped away his tangled sheets and took a running dive from his bedroom window down into the icy millpond.

In the next two days, while Keely found ways to visit Taylor and Quinn worked to finish Moriarity's wife's cherry buffet for her upcoming birthday, Blarney residents continued to bet feverishly on the Hart woman. Mac Flynn bet she could run ten miles in that long, free stride, and faster than any man in town. Mavis Kearney, at four feet ten and one half inches, declared the Hart woman was an "Amazon."

When Ophelia came to pick up Alfred from the all-male afternoon session at Blarney's pub, she beamed, announcing that the Hart woman had told her that she was staying for a few more days. The ladies of Hummingbird Lane would be having tomorrow's afternoon tea at the same time the men had an afternoon men-only "cool one"—a draft beer—at the pub. The men-only hour, from three to five every weekday afternoon, had incensed Taylor, Ophelia stated proudly. She added that Taylor Hart knew how to throw an elegant, steamy yet ladylike hissy fit, tossing in words like *male overlords, chauvinistic oinkers,* and *equal rights and opportunity of the sexes.*

"You could do with a haircut, Quinn Daniel," his mother had stated on the sixth day of Taylor's visit, when she picked up Keely for summer-vacation Bible school. "And a new shirt. Ah...have you thought of taking up jogging again? If you do, I'll see that one of your cousins comes over for Keely before dawn. My, wouldn't a morning run be refreshing? Just the way to start the day. Or maybe a run while the sun is setting. Uh...dear...do you think you could possibly win a race with the Hart woman?"

Quinn simmered under the taunts and questions and knew the town was squaring off, ready to begin betting.

Then Moriarity had stopped by, delivering planed wildcherry boards from his homestead's mill. "You're getting flabby, Quinn," he stated, looking at him critically. "Maybe you'd better think about taking up running. At dawn, maybe. Or sunset. You used to be pretty good. Better than the young ones nowadays. Timed yourself lately?"

Five

———

"I'm not anxious to sign the papers with Randolph Developers quickly, Mr. Jamison.... No, I am not trying to raise the price by putting you off," Taylor said between her teeth that same day. She glanced at the clock and frowned, realizing that she had allowed Jamison's two calls to intrude on her day. "Yes, I realize the profit that can be made from tourism, and at this point—" She paused, letting the effect sink into Jamison's brain, which she had begun to suspect was surrounded by a thick brick wall. "At this point, I am not doing business."

She frowned as he continued to toss out profit margins and possibilities, her fingers tightening on the telephone. She refused to be hassled into this decision. Her other hand played with the wide elastic bandage that she had used to wrap her breasts for running. Until she could shop for a sports bra, it would have to do. And it had proven quite comfortable. She'd missed running for the past few months, and now had seemed a good time to get back to the basic healthy schedule. Nothing was as glorious as running in

Blarney's morning mists, the damp air tingling on her skin. Then there was Maudie's grave and a quiet moment with her before returning to the house. "As I said, Mr. Jamison, our business for today is concluded."

She glanced at a small puppy lying in Maudie's herb garden, then pushed the disconnect button down. She plugged the new telephone cord into her computer. Within seconds, she had fired a message to her assistant that after this date anyone releasing her whereabouts or telephone number would answer to her.

Jamison's calls had cost her time from her busy schedule. Taylor glanced once at the teapots standing on the counter. The one shaped like a sitting elephant with a nose-spout and the one shaped like one of the unique nineteenth-century homes on Hummingbird Lane, should be handled carefully. There were the hummingbird and cardinal feeders, and Maudie's precious keepsakes, and her letters and journals. The rose garden needed fertilizing—with a blend of "manure tea," according to Maudie's directions.

Taylor studied the teapot that looked like a winking teddy bear and flipped on her computer again. She'd been in Blarney six days already and still hadn't begun her task. She typed in another electronic message—requesting an immediate vacation to care for personal business—to Max Winscott, chairman of the board.

Taylor checked the request, closed her eyes and typed, "Approximately one month. I will be available for immediate problems." Then she added, "Max, I need this," and sent the message.

Within minutes, Max Winscott's barroom voice crackled over the telephone. "You got it, Hart. Take as much time as you want. Hell, you haven't taken a real vacation in what— six, seven years? Just one question. Anything I can do?"

"Pray that I don't fall into any more blackberry bushes." Max's booming laughter caused her to smile.

Minutes later, Taylor crouched beside the black-brown-and-white puppy, who was enjoying bits of the Perkins's

eef roast mixed with water. The puppy's big brown ears
angled while he ate greedily, his white-tipped tail arching
ver his back. He didn't have a collar, and his ribs showed.
"Are you an orphan, boy?"

The wary, muddy puppy licked her hand and yipped sev-
ral times. "You've done a bit of damage, Digger," she
whispered, glancing at the dirty bones he had dug up and
gnawed. Since he knew the location of the soup bones, he
was probably the culprit who buried them. "No more of
hat while I'm here. You'll have plenty to eat...Digger.
That's your name unless someone claims you. You can stay
with me until I leave. Then we'll have to find you a home.
But remember...no more digging in Maudie's garden."

Later the puppy scampered at her heels while Taylor
walked along Ferguson Lake, following the rock pathway to
the old mill. When asked for the best craftsman to repair
antique furniture, Ophelia had recommended Quinn.
"Donovan again," Taylor murmured darkly, walking toward the millhouse and the man who had struck her on a
level no one else had dared. "Apparently he is the apple of
everyone's eye, Digger. A multi-talented genius with wood
or anything else he chooses."

A swan skimmed across the sunset reflected in the water,
and fluffy ducklings bobbed along, following their mother
into the bushes. The old walkway led to the arch of a small
wooden bridge, then to the open door of the mill.

Taylor smoothed the tight twist of her hair, then the tuck
of her long-sleeved blouse in her gray slacks. She'd plucked
thorns from these same clothes at dawn, concentrating on
them with a vengeance and reliving the whole incredible
scenario. Quinn was definitely too old to be playing games,
and she was too old to be stunned. Taylor flinched when she
felt a sharp, very familiar prick at her thigh. She found the
thorn and plucked it free. She threw it into the night, just as
she tossed away thoughts of being at Quinn's mercy.

She noted the small nubs on her sleeves. She'd only
brought along enough clothing for six days, and would have
to make purchases.

The soft, sweet night enveloped her as she walked to
ward the millhouse. There was no reason she shouldn't se
Quinn later than she had planned. Taylor glanced at th
lake, wishing for a sight of Baby, her Loch Ness monster
and trying to justify her evening visit to Quinn. There wa
absolutely no reason she shouldn't take her exercise on th
way to see a man she wanted to refinish Maudie's furni
ture. She'd managed difficult people and situations for eons
If Quinn had the necessary expertise, she would find a wa
to deal with him.

"Donovan?" she asked of the mill's looming shadows
Then, louder: "Donovan?" The only sound was the wate
from the creek falling musically into the pond.

Digger strolled to a towel lying on the floor, ploppe
down on it and went to sleep as if he were home.

The smell of wood tangled with the evening scents o
earth and plants. Taylor picked through the various scent
in the room—Italian seasoning, freshly cut wood, varnis
and oil, the musty scent of grain stacked against the wall
She lifted a child's ball, held it to her as she walked alon
one wall. Amid neatly arranged hand tools, a baby pictur
of Keely was tacked to the roughly planed lumber. A lon
work table was filled with jars of antique hinges, variou
wood glues, different-size clamps. A battered bookcase hel
worn books and layers of various wood veneers, and ram
bling shelves held various sizes of paint cans. An elegan
cherry buffet with claw feet stood apart, disdaining the hug
mill wheel. A small, delicate wooden dry sink without doo
was tucked in a corner.

There was another area for an elaborate tiny castle just b
enough for a child, made of plywood and boxes. Keely's ra
doll flopped out a turret window. Next to it, a large dol
house stood on a battered picnic table. Bits of paper, fat
ric, glue and scissors rested throughout the tiny room:
Taylor studied the unique design of the cathedral ceiling
the layout of the rooms, and realized that whoever ha
made it had an uncommon knowledge of architecture.

Through a long, wide window, the sunset settled into the huge, airy room, brushing a wide slanted-top table. An architect's pencils and long rolls of paper lay over a drawing of a large multipurpose building. Taylor frowned, tracing the layout. If this was Quinn's work, he was excellent, more than that, creative.

Her fingertip wandered to a four-leaf clover lying in a tiny china saucer. She smiled gently, and touched the rumpled tape that added the fourth leaf to the natural three. "I love my Daddy," Keely had written on the big lines of her paper. Low in one torn corner, she had attempted "Tay."

Taylor slowly traced the oversized, childish scrawl, and she smiled, thinking of Keely.

Then a large, tanned hand abruptly pushed hers away. The scents of soap and Quinn swirled around her as his tall body heated her back. "My daughter isn't up to playing games, Hart," he said slowly, the deep, raspy tone reminding her of a growling warlock disturbed in his lair.

She turned then, taking her time, gearing up for Quinn looming over her. Shadows swallowed the room now, and the crickets and frogs were beginning their chorus. The light coming from the open doorway behind Quinn outlined his bare shoulders.

"Quinn," she said simply, and wished her voice hadn't come out as a husky sigh. "I...uh..."

Taylor promised herself she would not look beyond his bare throat. Water dripped from Quinn's hair, beading his shoulders. She followed a drop that shimmered and slowly fell to the hair on his chest. Her fingertips flexed, wanting to rummage through the dark nest. "I...uh..." Taylor Hart, CEO, tough negotiator, never stammered, she reminded herself as Quinn leaned closer. He braced his weight against the table, placing one hand on either side of her hips.

A drop of water fell between them, startling her, and she jumped.

She leaned back, reached out a hand for support, and found his warm, callused one wrapped around hers. Quinn leaned closer, his eyes narrowing, the dim light slashing across his cheekbones and his nose. "So the lady has come calling again. What do you want this time, Tay?"

The husky, sensual tone raised the hair on the back of her neck. She thought of Quinn's stunning light kiss and wondered if another would create the same magic. She cleared her throat, damned Jamison's call for making her late and tried to force her eyes away from Quinn's lips, which flirted with laughter. "Ah...I meant to call.... Then it was too late and I decided to walk—" She caught her breath, scrambling for control. "It's about Maudie's furniture. Moriarity tells me you can love a piece of furniture back into health. The...uh...spool-leg table needs tightening and...uh...the veneer on the headboard in her guest bedroom is beginning to crack...."

She swallowed again, aware now that his thumb caressed her palm. His hands were rough, broad, safe. "You've just had a shower, haven't you? Oh...sorry to... Ah...where's Keely?" she managed, her eyes dropping to Quinn's broad damp chest.

She closed her eyes and inhaled. Quinn Donovan's male scent dominated the lighter ones of soap and baby powder. What did Keely call it? Fairy dust?

The air between Quinn and herself sizzled, stabbed with tiny lightning bolts. Quinn, looking tense and fierce, reached past her to turn the intercom button marked Keely's Room. He listened a moment, his eyes locked with Taylor's, then he studied the shape of her mouth. "Keely's dreaming of catching her leprechauns. She fancies claiming you as her mother. I see our local puppy has already made your acquaintance."

"Digger? Do you know who owns him?"

"Digger suits him. He's a beagle runt. Not good for hunting or breeding. He comes here for a bit, then wanders off. He's the town puppy, and he hasn't chosen who to claim."

Taylor wasn't thinking about the puppy as Quinn added softly, "I'm wearing a towel, Tay. There's no need to blush."

Her lower back met the edge of the drawing board as he moved against her. The towel dampened her slacks, and the folded bulk at his waist pressed into her stomach.

The hard thrust of his thighs met hers, and a shiver ran through her. She wanted to move away; her legs didn't respond. Quinn's damp chest pressed lightly against her breasts, and he inhaled, just once. He rubbed from side to side, like a great untamed beast luxuriating in a soft nest. Then again, very slowly. "Are you going to kiss me or not?" he demanded, jerking her against him.

"If you think—" Taylor pushed against his flat stomach, and the towel unfurled in her fingers. Her eyes widened; the weight of the damp towel tugged at her trembling fingers.

Quinn smoothed her back slowly. The smile that had been lurking on his lips spread into his eyes. "So here we are, Tay."

"The door on Maudie's china cabinet is loose, and there is a scratch on the dresser, and..." She rambled on helplessly, her fists clenching the towel.

Quinn bent and nuzzled her nose with his, stunning her. Her stomach lurched, and her thighs felt like warm, pliant putty. "Maudie wanted her things close to her. She wanted everything to be in her home and in its place, Tay," he said gently. "I made do, but the furniture should be brought here, where the repairs can be done properly."

Taylor cleared her throat, aware that her fists—filled with the towel—were lodged against Quinn's damp, hard hips. His eyes went slowly from hers to her hands, resting trembling against him, then back again. Locking her gaze with his, drowning her in the sultry promise of his meadow green eyes, Quinn traced her lips with the tip of his tongue.

Little kept her from launching herself at him. From dragging his mouth to hers. From dropping the towel and... "You've got the job," she whispered unevenly, and hoped the shadows would hide her flush.

If ever she wanted to toss a man over her shoulder and run into her cave, this was that moment.

Taylor inhaled, summoning a tight, cold smile. Quinn grinned widely as she kept her eyes locked on his and tucked the towel around his hips. Her fingers met his arousal—there was no denying the steely outline—and Quinn's expression jerked to a frown. His hand covered hers, flattening her palm against him. "Tay," he said roughly, breathing unevenly. He released her hand, giving her a choice. "You could stay."

Her fingertips hovered over the shape of him before Taylor jerked her hand away, rubbing it against the other.

"I . . . uh . . . should be going." She nodded briskly, and prayed her legs wouldn't buckle when she walked away from him.

When she thought she heard him chuckle, she pivoted, the hairs on the back of her neck lifting. "What?"

Quinn tilted his head to one side and crossed his arms over his chest. His teeth gleamed in the dim light, his grin widening as she walked back to him. "I'll give you something to laugh about, Donovan," she stated tightly.

"I doubt it," he murmured very seriously.

His damp hair curled between her fingers as she dragged him down to her mouth. Quinn's face was hard and rough beneath her palms, and she could have spent a lifetime exploring his rough warm skin, the hard, thrusting bones. "Here. Laugh about this."

Green eyes narrowed as she neared, closing her eyes and pushing her lips against his. His mouth was firm, warm, against hers, offering nothing. Taylor jerked back, waiting, daring him. "You're out of practice, Tay," Quinn murmured easily, humor lurking in his tone. Then he took her mouth, sweetly, coaxingly, magically.

He shifted, and Taylor locked her arms around him, seeking that gentle magic. It slid into hunger as Quinn's lips eased hers slightly apart, his tongue caressing her lips gently, flicking at them. She sank into the scent of him, the textures, the heat flowing in them, around them. The rising hunger stunned her, and she could not resist.

Quinn shuddered, his kisses gentling as he eased her away from him, his features taut in the shadows. For a full heartbeat, Taylor's warring emotions swirled around her.

Then she gave in to the one she knew best. She gathered her control around her like a cape and walked away.

Digger yipped once and followed her.

Four days later, Quinn and Moriarity eased the antique dresser down the stairs and through Maudie's front door. It was not an easy task, considering that Taylor was stretching her long legs, limbering up for her morning run. Quinn was jealous of whatever was binding her breasts. The thought almost caused him to drop his end of the dresser. With three long, sleepless nights behind him, those lightly tanned, smoothly muscled legs were not helping his concentration as they maneuvered the heavy dresser into his pickup.

At Taylor's side, a young executive type with designer sunglasses and a fake tan was carrying on a laughing, flirtatious dialogue. His stylish haircut marked him as an alien to the laid-back rural community. His running shoes probably cost more than Quinn made in a month, if people paid him in cash alone.

Tied to a shady tree, Digger yipped and chewed on an assortment of newly purchased puppy toys. Looking at the puppy, Moriarity wiped the sweat from his forehead. "Looks like that runt has found a home. She's taken him to the vet's. Asked Wilbur about housebreaking him—a beagle. No one in these parts housebreaks a beagle or a running hound."

"She's not from these parts," Quinn muttered as Taylor bent to rub Digger's belly and her shorts tightened over her hips.

The executive turned his head toward Taylor, and Quinn recognized the contemplative, pointy-eared hungry-male look. He gripped the claw-shaped foot of the dresser and wondered how well the boy could catch it.

The first week of June was hot. Well, so was he, Quinn thought darkly, and wondered how he could take the duration of Taylor's visit. With an under-thirty-year-old junior executive sizing up Taylor's backside, Quinn realized he had just experienced his first round of jealousy.

Junior probably hadn't noted Taylor's loose shirt. At the moment, there wasn't anything to notice. The thought of her wrapping and flattening her breasts drove Quinn's temperature higher. He decided the action bordered on the criminal, and began fantasizing about unraveling her. That led to other steamy thoughts, and a hard ache low in his belly. The few quick laps he'd taken in the freezing millpond hadn't trimmed the heat within him.

The nightmares that had stopped long ago now swept into his sleep. The building crumbling slowly, an injured workman lying in the hospital, Nancy screaming and shaking Keely. Then there was the need to draw, to make a building come to life with his sketches. Whatever roamed within him, the restless need to create was stirred by Taylor's presence. She challenged him, made him ache for something too dangerous—for the dreams he'd locked away.

He could manage to survive without tasting Taylor... maybe.... All he had to do was stop breathing.

"City slicker," Moriarty muttered about the man wearing the latest brand-name jogging gear and stretching his legs at Taylor's side. He posed and flexed, and Quinn wanted to invite him into the backyard for an education on poaching. Moriarty continued, "Madge says a city feller placed a long call to the Hart woman—Keely's 'Tay'—two days ago, then again last night. Maybe he's her feller. You ever notice how flat the woman is?"

"No," Quinn snapped, glaring at Moriarty. He wondered how many other men were watching Taylor's flat chest, especially when her T-shirt was damp with sweat. He glanced at Junior, gauging the smoothly balanced muscles developed by regular gym workouts. Taylor caught Quinn's look. Her face paled and tightened beneath her headband.

Her hair shimmered blue-black in the sun, drawn high upon her head.

"Whew," Moriarity whispered as they tied a rope around the dresser. "That was a nasty look she gave you, boyo. Raked you over the coals. What have you done to get her dander up?"

Hers? Every muscle in his body ached. If he didn't find out what flattened her, he'd—

"Mind your own business," Quinn returned absently, studying Taylor's smoothly rounded backside. The loose legs of her shorts fluttered enticingly over the curve of her bottom, allowing him a view. He stopped and pivoted to Moriarity, whose eyes were narrowed on Taylor. "Did you give her the file I prepared about Blarney Flats?"

Moriarity continued to stare, nodded, then punched the buttons on his stopwatch. "From the bridge over the creek to Flynn's bakery... five seconds..."

He glanced at Quinn. "Yep. Man. That woman is lean. Built like a boy. Not much bounce. Gave the file to her just after she reported that the men-only hour was outrageous. She wanted me to do something about sexism in Blarney Flats. Said she would if I didn't. The woman won't go down easy, when it comes to push and shove. One of the ladies on Hummingbird Lane said that the delivery truck stopped in front of Maudie's house with an armload of mail-order parcels. Boy, are you feeling all right?"

When Quinn ignored him, the sheriff studied the runners. "The fancy-pants boy is soft. She's pacing her stride to his. She can take him. Outdistance him easy. Bet he can't make four miles at her side. What do you think, boyo?"

Quinn didn't want to think about the man making anything with Taylor. Or jogging beside her. What if whatever was holding her breasts came unfurled? At close range, Taylor's new friend would see every jiggle and curve. The thought of another man frothing at the mouth over Taylor's body made him want to... "Stand here and gossip if you want, Moriarity. But I've got work to do."

"Ah! Painting the gingerbread trim and delivering your daughter to her all-day—slumber?—birthday party at the Flynns." Quinn's cousin grinned. "Guess that will leave a long, lonely night, eh, boyo?"

That night, Quinn ate at the pub, ignoring Lilian Orson's blatant invitations and brooding over Taylor's fluttering shorts and whatever was flattening her breasts. In search of husband number five, Lilian had decided that Quinn suited her perfectly. Quinn studied Lilian's top-heavy, lushly structured body and decided that in the space of ten days he'd come to prefer Taylor's lean look. He was just finishing his meal when Taylor and her "jogger friend" strolled in, their heads close together as they laughed.

Quinn stared darkly at her, noting the dimples she had dragged out for Junior.

Taylor's gypsy mane tumbled around her face, gold hoops shining at her ears. Buttoned up the front, her long, straight dress clung and molded long, curving legs. Scraps of red leather and heels served as shoes.

Quinn placed his fork aside, his hands flat to the table. Dangerous and red, the dress could make a man froth at the mouth and howl at the moon.

He stared at her breasts, taking in the shape of them. She wore some damnable lingerie that raised and thrust them against the red cloth. The two small, enticing mounds shifted beneath the material, and Quinn scowled. The pert shape made a man want to rip away the dress.

The red folds swirled around her shapely legs, and Quinn forced himself to swallow.

On Taylor's long, elegant body, the dress was a pure, undiluted invitation. *She should be wearing the . . . whatever . . . that flattened her,* Quinn decided darkly.

Then there was a drift of shadowing on her lids, serving to darken, slant and mystify her eyes. The red lip gloss was sinful and inviting.

Quinn remembered her lying drowsy and warm in the big brass bed. He remembered her untutored kiss. He glanced around the pub and found the men drooling, the women scowling.

Lilian slid into Quinn's booth unnoticed while he concentrated on the man's hand latched to Taylor's waist. He decided darkly that the hand rode much too low, and found himself surging from the booth.

"Donovan," Taylor said softly, warily, as he pushed aside Frank Davis, a Flynn cousin, on his way toward her. She glanced at Lilian, who now hovered at Quinn's side.

He nodded at Taylor, sizing up the man, who was dressed in a loose designer shirt and slacks and thin Italian loafers. He stared down at the man's sockless feet and knew he wasn't from backwoods Arkansas, where men wore boots in pubs. "Hart, who's this?" he demanded.

She inhaled, and Donovan noted the soft red dress, the snug fit of it over her breasts. "Why are you wearing a dress?" he demanded, incensed that she would dress like a *femme fatale* for Junior.

She should be wearing her flattening thing. Quinn refused to think of what covered her hips. If it matched her bra, it would be skimpy. Probably high around her thighs and little enough of it—

Taylor's mouth tightened, and her stormy eyes skipped down Quinn's loosely buttoned cotton shirt, worn jeans and boots. "Donovan. This is John Morgan. John, this is Quinn Donovan. Handyman. Miller. Housepainter. There. Now that the introductions are completed, if you'll just move out of our way, Quinn—"

"Not just yet." So she didn't mind this man's lily white hands roaming over her body, did she? She'd run from the touch of *his* hands. Were they too rough, too poor to touch her? Resenting his anger, Quinn shrugged off Lilian's cautioning touch. He allowed his gaze to deliberately saunter down Taylor's rigid body, then pushed his lips into a challenging, tight smile.

Taylor lowered her brows, her voice low and precise. "The reason I'm wearing this dress—since you asked me so nicely—is that we are here to have dinner, Quinn. Cade said that this is corned-beef-and-cabbage night, and that the pub serves the best. But if you need manners served up on a plate instead, I imagine I could take care of the matter."

Quinn wondered how precisely Taylor would act if he had to remove Mr. Lily-White's hands from her waist.

John's frown jumped from Taylor's set face to Quinn's rigid one. "Look, if there's a problem, Taylor, we can discuss the land development some other time."

Quinn pulled his lips back from his teeth in a wolfish smile. In another minute, he would toss the little slime back into his custom gray sports car. "Yes. Do that."

"Quinn," Taylor warned, pushing his stomach with the flat of her hand. "Back off."

Quinn's fingers circled her wrist and brought her palm to his mouth for a kiss. He wanted the wimp to know that Taylor Hart was claimed by one Quinn Donovan. John's face went white as Quinn took a step toward him.

"A five on Quinn," someone whispered, and Quinn jerked his stare from John's to see Blarney Pub's best watching the scene.

"No takers," someone flipped back. "Quinn's got him. Solid muscle against city flab. That, and Quinn's Osage-Russian blood is showing. Can't say as I've ever seen him that worked up."

"The tyke could be faster."

"Nah. No bets. Quinn's hot to brawl. Saw him once at eighteen . . . had that same expression . . . took five big ya-hoos. . . . Can't say I've seen that look on his face since. . . ." The discussion dropped when Quinn leveled his scowl at them.

"You're making a scene," Taylor hissed, trying his grip. He held her slender wrist gently, firmly, just as he would hold her when they were alone. She shimmered with anger; it clung to her like a brewing thunderstorm, ready to strike. "At your age, you should try a little dignity."

"Dignity be damned," he muttered, wanting to pick her up and run into the woods with her.

"If you'd run with her every day, Quinn," someone called, "she wouldn't be looking for other partners."

"You're coming with me, Tay," Quinn said between his teeth, aching for John to deny him.

Taylor eased her wrist away from Quinn. "Call me tomorrow, John," she said, without releasing Quinn's stare. "I'm sorry for this intrusion, but perhaps tonight isn't the best time for our discussion."

"Taylor, I'll just wait for you in the car." While not abandoning her totally to Quinn, John melted and sniveled away. Blarney's best barely missed him as they focused on Quinn and Taylor, who raised her head.

"Yes, John. You do that. I've changed my mind. I'll just be a minute here. Then we can go to dinner elsewhere." She glanced at the curious crowd, tossed her head and ordered, "Into my office, Donovan," before she walked to open the nearest door. When he entered, she locked it behind him.

"Donovan . . ." Taylor said a moment later, clearly trying to control her temper. She tried again, "Donovan, just exactly what were you doing out there?"

He leaned against the wall, watching the dress open and close along her legs as she strode back and forth. "If you're making deals about Ferguson Lake, perhaps you'd better let the townspeople know the terms," he said darkly. He didn't want to account for the dark anger. When he saw another man touch her, it had leaped and swept through him like a mountain fire.

She pivoted, facing him. Her legs braced apart, tightening the red material. A light behind her outlined those legs, and Quinn's mouth went dry. "I am a businesswoman, listening and weighing all the options."

"The hell you are," he returned. "Junior was all over you."

Her eyes widened, then narrowed with anger. She swallowed and said between tight lips, "I won't dignify that. John is a representative of a firm, and I am listening to a business proposition.'' She scowled at Quinn's lifted eye-brow.

A knock on the door preceded Lilian's muffled "Quinn, honey, it's Lilian. Are you all right?'' There was a round of muffled guffaws, then silence.

"We're in a business conference, Lilian," Quinn drawled.

Taylor flicked a dark look at the door. "Quinn, honey, who is Lilian?'' she asked, too sweetly.

When he didn't answer, she surged ahead, "So. Quinn, explain your outlandish behavior.'' She flicked her hand impatiently. "This macho male garbage... Go ahead, I don't have all day. At any minute, Lilian honey may be breaking down the door to rescue you.''

Her glance slowly ran over the small, spotless room, with its sink and porcelain fixtures. Her mouth parted and her eyes widened at the graffiti etched on the scrubbed walls. She closed her lids and slowly shook her head, as though wishing a bad nightmare away. "We're in the men's room," she whispered shakily. Then, more firmly: "*I'm* in the men's room of a pub!''

Her shocked expression swept away the last of Quinn's anger. "Yes, Tay," he said patiently, pushing back a grin. "You've dragged me into the men's room...where *I* have a perfect right to be.''

She sagged against a wall, ran her hand over her fore-head and stared at him blankly. "I never react this way. I'm always in control. I think I need to sit down.''

"Not in here, Tay. I'll rescue you," Quinn offered gal-lantly before he unlocked the door and swept her up into his arms.

His mind raced as he opened the door and eased her carefully through it. To be fair, she wasn't the only one in the men's room with regrets. He'd acted like a bully. Tay-lor's lingerie and red dress had acted like a red flag to a charging bull.

The knowledge that no other woman had caused these emotions did little for his shaky control.

He'd barely reined his desire to make love to her there, against a graffiti-etched wall. But he wanted her in a soft bed, with time for magic and sweet kisses. When they made love, he wanted her to choose him.

When he took Taylor, he wanted her to see him coming. To understand that she couldn't walk away easily.

Quinn frowned. Whatever had driven him to rip her away from Mr. Lily-White would cost him dearly. Blarney residents would have something new to gossip over, much better than the Flynn cow that had just wandered into a Donovan cornfield. The matter of Quinn rising to the bait over a woman would delight the community.

He gathered Taylor closer, nuzzling the soft, sweet mane of curls and thinking of waking up to her tangled with him. Quinn inhaled sharply. Around Taylor, his state of arousal seemed permanent. Once he got her to safety, he'd face Blarney's best with an offer to meet anyone behind the building at the first snicker. Meanwhile, the drape of her skirt served nicely to shield his painfully tightened body.

"This is your fault, Donovan," the woman in his arms murmured hollowly.

Quinn slid his hand beneath her hair, cupping the back of her head. He pushed her face against his throat, protecting her from the crowd's curiosity. "She's not feeling well. Too much heat. Business pressure. Change of climate," he explained, carrying her through the pub.

Moriarty's low guffaw followed them into the night.

Six

At eleven-thirty that night, Taylor unlocked Maudie's front door. She closed it too hard, then placed her hand flat on the old oval glass, willing it not to shatter.

Digger was silent, and Taylor eased her way to the back porch to find him sleeping soundly. The puppy stirred on his new bed—a thick towel—and Taylor returned to the parlor and her thoughts of one Quinn Donovan. She gritted her teeth when she remembered the way Quinn had easily lifted her into John's front seat. "Take her. She's all yours," he had said.

As if she were a car and he were handing over the title to a new buyer. She would love to rip Quinn to shreds.

When John, a representative of Randolph Developers, had offered dinner that afternoon, she'd accepted. Business dinners were familiar, soothing territory. She understood the rules. Light, easy talk, gradually taking the main points home. Safe, verbal fencing, give-and-take. John came from a world that she knew and understood. After

Quinn's earth-shattering kiss in the mill, she'd needed the familiar ground.

The dress was an experiment, a pick-me-up. She'd wanted to see if John reacted to her as a woman. Her hand skimmed down the red-hot dress. The lingerie, a spicy yet conservative peachy-beige set, matched the dress's sexy-female nuances.

Taylor blinked. *What was she doing?* She'd always been so complete, so controlled. She dressed for comfort, travel and business. She preferred travels-well, looks-good business dress, in grays, navy blues and blacks.

She also preferred good basic business-look earrings, if any. But once the dress was on, swishing and clinging to create a startling, leggy look, Maudie's antique hoops had been too delicious to resist.

Just like Quinn. Something about him—arrogance, heat, whatever—demanded that she take him down a notch on some basic level. Not that she had experience on basic levels. Or wanted it until now. Holding her own with Quinn was essential. A matter of pride.

When he'd studied her breasts earlier in the evening, boldly tracing the shape with his eyes and staring at her as if she'd committed a crime, Taylor's whole body had tightened into one sensitive knot.

Quinn had left no doubt as to his attraction to her. Or his dislike. She returned the emotions, doubling them. She'd known him exactly ten days, and he'd caught her broadside, turning her safe world upside down.

Then Keely had skipped into her heart. She was everything a little girl should be—her world safe and perfect, filled with giggles and fairy tales and love.

Taylor scanned Hummingbird Lane, knowing that everyone was where they should be at midnight. Safe. Warm. Close to loved ones. Everyone was just exactly where they should be…except her. She had what she wanted—no ties, no permanent home, not even a car to infringe on her traveling life-style.

But did she *really* have what she wanted?

She shivered, though the summer night was warm and filled with the scent of honeysuckle and roses and newly cut hay. Crickets chirped, frogs croaked, and she hoped the baby Loch Ness was safe.

John suited her world. He was a skilled negotiator, pointing out pluses and minimizing minuses and listing high profits. In precise business language, he described plans for a sprawling condominium and golf course, country living for the wealthy.

Taylor inhaled, studying the stars. She really didn't like the development picture John had painted. Nor did she like the reflection of herself in his eyes, the easy certainty that she would want to turn a quick, neat profit, despite the dangers to the community.

The magic that was Blarney Flats wrapped around her. A baby Loch Ness and a delicate ecology that let the unique shad live untouched, when they could live nowhere else ... where puppies claimed strangers for their own, where elderly "folks" were treasured and a little girl named Keely wanted a leprechaun to grant her a mommy.

Then there was Quinn.

Savage. Beast. Jerk. He'd stuffed her into John's car as though she were a child instead of a grown woman. In the rearview mirror, Quinn's arrogant stance—hands on hips, hair lifting with the breeze—had raised her hackles.

Taylor stalked into the parlor, tossing her purse and the developer's plans that John had given her on the doily-covered table. She kicked off her shoes and stripped away the dress, throwing it over the banister and taking the stairs two at a time. In the morning, she'd find Donovan and cut him down to size.

Taylor took the last step and rounded the corner, concentrating on just how she would burn Donovan's well-developed backside.

Maudie's big brass bed stood in the moonlight, the curtains fluttering in the night breeze. A noise took Taylor's eyes searching the shadows, where Quinn Donovan sat, rocking Keely in his arms.

"Nice outfit." His raw, deep voice spread over the easy sounds of the night coming from the open window.

Taylor glanced down at herself and gasped.

Winscott's cool lady CEO actually issued a certified old-fashioned gasp. She dealt with that fact while she grabbed a lacy curtain she'd been mending from the end of the bed and held it in front of her, peering at Quinn.

Maudie's big maple rocker creaked as Quinn continued rocking his daughter, his shoes discarded. The gentle night wind fluttered the curtains riding along his bare shoulder. Keely was wearing his shirt over a short nightie with ruffled panties. When she stirred restlessly, Quinn tucked his shirt closer to her. "You've taken your own sweet time," he said darkly. Then: "She was playing outside at Mother's and saw you in his car. She was afraid you were leaving," he said simply, his tone hushed. "Nothing would satisfy her. So I brought her here, and we waited."

The little girl sniffed and cuddled in Quinn's arms. Taylor forgot why she'd been running up the stairs, why she was so angry with Quinn. She smoothed Keely's damp cheek. "She's been crying."

In the shadows, Quinn's face was hard, shadowed by his beard. His hair stood out, as though combed by impatient fingers. He inhaled slowly, easing Keely against him. "Keely thinks she is responsible for you leaving town... that somehow she did something wrong and you went away with the man. She thinks my ex-wife is dead and that she somehow caused her death. Nancy—Keely's mother—is very much alive. I haven't found a way to tell her that her mother didn't want her."

"And you did want her," Taylor added softly, searching his eyes. She smoothed Keely's jumbled hair back from her forehead. "What happened?"

Keely hugged Queenie close and sighed against Quinn's chest. He checked to see if she was sleeping deeply, then nuzzled her short, riotous curls. "She's mine now. I found her mother shaking her badly when she was just two months old. Nancy was screaming, furious that she'd conceived, hating the baby and me." He closed his eyes wearily and leaned back against the rocker.

"So you brought Keely here, to Blarney and your family, where she'd be safe . . . where she'd have loving family and caring baby-sitters while you worked," Taylor whispered, wishing fiercely that nothing could ever hurt Keely.

Something tight unfurled within Taylor as she looked at Quinn. Filling the old rocker, sprawled to accommodate his daughter tucked against his chest, Quinn looked like any anxious father, lines etched across his forehead and around his mouth. She found her hand curled in his. "You'll find a way to tell her when it's time," Taylor said, knowing it was true. Donovan was the kind of man who did his best for those he loved. "You're not all bad, Donovan."

"You're not, either, Hart," he whispered, catching her hand and turning his face into it. "You're like Maudie in some ways—doing the best you can . . . tending strays and lonely children and having tea with lonely people who have been forgotten. You care for people, Tay." His kiss branded her palm, tore away her anger, tossing it into the moonlight.

She forced herself to breathe as his eyes lingered on the lace covering her. Taylor glanced down. The lace curtain shielded nothing, clearly revealing her lingerie and the dark band supporting her thigh-high stockings.

"Did you kiss him?" he demanded, holding her hand to his cheek.

She tilted her head, the humiliating scene in the pub springing to life once more. A kiss from John would have all the enchantment of cold fried eggs, while Quinn's promised heaven and heat and a safe harbor when the storms calmed. *Why had she let Quinn step into her life?* "I don't see that it's any of your business. John is a nice man. And unlike you, Donovan, he has manners."

He scowled up at her, his fingers tightening, lacing with hers. His broad, rough palm met hers, callused and warm. "I never claimed to be nice, Tay. Save the manners for Mr. Lily-White. I asked you if you kissed him."

Taylor tried to tug her hand away. "Listen, boyo, I am an adult—"

Keely stirred in his arms as Quinn jerked Taylor's hand nearer, his expression fierce. "Daddy? Tay?" Then Keely lurched from Quinn's arms and wrapped hers around Taylor. "Tay, you came back!"

"I feel a little like Lassie," Taylor whispered shakily as she gathered Keely close. The little girl settled on her hip; the soft drape of the sleepy child's body was welcome after Quinn's nettling arrogance.

Quinn snorted and rose to his full height, towering over Taylor. Keely's fingers toyed with Taylor's hair, and Taylor rocked her. The child was lovable, cuddly, but Quinn's dark, hard scowl was another matter. "That red dress you had on probably has Blarney's young bloods calling Madge for your telephone number right now."

She looked over Keely's curls. She tried not to look down the rippling muscles as he stretched, arms overhead, his aura dangerously male in the small, frilly room. She refused to tug the curtain higher, where Keely's weight had pulled it from her breasts. "I wear what I want, Donovan."

"You caused a scene," he returned, showing his teeth. His tone was just above a growl.

"*I* caused one?" She kept her voice hushed, though she wanted to yell. She never yelled.

Quinn smirked, a gleam of teeth against his dark stubble. He'd gotten to her. Tempted to argue, Taylor refused to discuss the matter with Keely in her arms. Instead, she murmured, very properly, "Your daughter is very lovable, Donovan. Unlike someone I know."

He trailed a fingertip down her cheek, and Taylor resented the instant warmth in its path. "Lovable. Now there's a word for a child, or a snugly pet between the blankets." *Not for what passes between a man and a woman.*

She shivered as the fingertip slid across her lips, tugging gently as he leaned closer. Then Quinn reached for his daughter gently. "Come on now, my little fairy princess," he said to Keely. "Now that the frog prince has returned your Tay, we can go home to feed your purple dragon. That is, if we can escape the trolls that wait under the bridge."

Keely giggled and launched herself at Quinn, who caught her neatly. "She came back, Daddy. Can we have her now?"

But Quinn's gaze was slowly traveling down, then up, Taylor's body. Before she could catch her breath or snatch the blasted slipping curtain, he bent to kiss her. Then, for good measure, Keely gave her a juicy kiss, too. "Take me to my castle, fair prince," the little girl ordered majestically, tapping Quinn's broad shoulder. "With fairy dust protecting us, we shall return tomorrow to save the queen from the dragon."

She grinned hopefully at Taylor. "Unless I can sleep with you, Tay."

Looming over Taylor, the hem of a lace curtain fluttering on one broad shoulder, Quinn inhaled sharply, his eyes fierce with hunger as he said, "Oh, no, my fairy princess. I must take you home, where tomorrow we will feast upon the long tails of the willow-walk fern."

"Spaghetti!" Keely cheered. She swung to Taylor with a yawn and rubbed her eyes with her fist. "You could come with us, Tay. Then you wouldn't be alone. My daddy can sprinkle fairy dust on you before you sleep and you'll be safe all night long. When you get scared of dragons and bears at night, my daddy hunts 'em."

Taylor had glimpsed what Quinn was hunting. A tiny curl of fire settled in her body as he stared at her breasts and lower. "I'll stay here, Keely. I'll be here in the morning. You have my word that I won't leave just yet," Taylor whispered, meaning it. Keely looked at her with troubled eyes, then curled against Quinn, holding him tightly. Over her head, Quinn's eyes met Taylor's. His hunger slammed into her, winding her, as she moved away, her hand over her racing heart.

From the back porch, Digger began a series of high-pitched barks, and Taylor's heart lurched with each one.

"Rabbit," Quinn explained roughly, his eyes sweeping over her. "Digger is 'sounding,' wanting to get on the trail."

While Digger's yips continued long into the night, Taylor thought of the kisses—Quinn's laced with hunger, Keely's with joy.

She listened to the puppy. The veterinarian had explained the runt had escaped death by fleeing a local "dog man" who wanted healthy "running dogs." Digger's high-pitched yelps didn't annoy Taylor; they sounded familiar and comforting, like the noises of the loving family she wished for and never had.

Just before she slept, Taylor heard a noise. Out on the lake, the very deepest safest place, Taylor thought she heard the baby Loch Ness purring among his friendly shad, swishing his grand tail and settling in for another fifty or so years.

"You're late, Hart," Quinn stated as his bicycle pulled beside her on the sidewalk the next morning. He watched her chest intently. Taylor was very glad the wide elastic bandage didn't reveal the tightening of her breasts. He continued to study her shape, though she shot him a warning frown.

"Stop it," she ordered beneath her breath. "Donovan, you are staring."

Dressed in a yellow shorts set that matched the bow in Quinn's hair, Keely grinned from her perch behind him. "Hi, Tay. I'm Daddy's scout. When you passed the stop sign, I told him to go."

Quinn's bland look was too innocent. He wasn't letting last night pass, or the storms between them, either.

"Good morning, Keely." Taylor hesitated, unused to anyone sharing her morning runs, the times when she did her best thinking. She decided instantly that she would speak to Keely and not to her father. Being carried through the pub and into the street, then tucked into a car like a child, still nettled. She pushed aside her lapse of control and the disgusting memory that she had given Quinn a dressing-down in a men's room.

She would set him straight no matter where she found
him, she corrected a second later.

She flicked a disdainful look at his morning beard, his
hair flowing on his shoulders. The tattered T-shirt did little
to hide his tanned chest, and there was blue and yellow paint
splattered on his worn cutoffs. But the long, masculine legs
stopped her breath. Quinn lifted his brows inquiringly, a
smile curving his lips. "Sleep well?" he asked pleasantly.

She wouldn't let him know that she'd crunched her pillow savagely beneath her and dreamed of his sweet, beguiling kisses, and of his hunger. That she'd fallen off the bed,
tangled in the sheets and the quilt, and awoken with a bump.
That she'd spent an hour on her back porch, curled up and
talking to the puppy. "Extremely well."

"Tay, will you be here today and tomorrow?" Keely
asked uncertainly.

"Yes, I will. And you're stuck with me for about another three weeks, Keely. I hope you'll stop by when you
can."

The little girl grinned. "Daddy, Tay jiggles when she
runs," Keely said thoughtfully as she studied Taylor's
shorts. "Will I, when I grow up?"

He chuckled, then shot Taylor a sizzling look. "We'll
have to see. Did I ever tell you the story about the elf who
wanted to race a bunny?" he asked as he swung the bicycle
toward Molly's house.

Two hours later, Taylor said, "You can't hide behind
Keely now, Quinn. Cade said she's spending the day at her
grandmother's." He stopped smoothing tung oil on Maudie's
small walnut chest and turned to find Taylor standing behind him.

She'd come straight from her morning shower, dressed in
jeans and a light T-shirt, her damp hair curling around her
face. Her head went up as he leaned against his work
counter. He closed the tung oil can and turned to her slowly.

The new jeans fit in all the right places, the lemony T-shirt
tucked neatly into her slender, belted waist. Her breasts

lifted as she inhaled, her eyes daring him. Quinn remembered the softness of her skin, the tender shape of her breasts. He regretted whatever new torture she was wearing beneath the T-shirt. It meant he would be matching styles and colors of sexy bras and briefs in his dreams.

Her eyes ripped down him, then back up. "Don't you have any clothes without holes? Maybe you'd better work on your upward-mobility wardrobe, Quinn."

He'd been working in his cutoff shorts and nothing else, wrapping the cool shadows and gentle sounds of the mill around him. Hungry for Taylor, her scents and her intriguing dimple, he'd sketched a bit, feeling out the paper, feeling the shape of the building coming to life under his pencil—taking the image from his brain and running it into his fingers. Creating was what he knew, what roamed inside him, taunting him. He'd sacrificed everything for an exciting career, working days without rest to see a sketch come to life.

And then everything had been shattered with the collapse of the building, the threats of lawsuits. One day, he'd been a successful, innovative architect, the next, he'd been scrambling in an intricate legal hassle. Back then, he'd known that any wrong step would take his daughter from him. For months he had walked a tight, deadly line, filled with nightmares.

Taylor brought it all back to him, slapped him in the face with his fears and challenged him on every level.

"You'd better cool off," he offered mildly, realizing that of all the moments Taylor could have picked to chastise him, this was the worst. He'd been sticking to his corner, minding his furniture and trying not to think of her.

The sight of her standing in front of the big brass bed, the frilly bits of lingerie clinging, barely concealing, had remained with him throughout the night. A two-o'clock cold shower hadn't cooled his need to sink deep in Taylor, to lock on to her storms and ride them out with her.

"I want to know why you acted like a savage at the pub. A real jerk," she demanded, her eyes widening as they swept slowly down and discovered the tightening of his shorts. She stepped back and jerked her eyes back to his face. "Don't let it happen again."

His constantly aroused state around Taylor annoyed Quinn, her startled flush raising his temperature. "What?" he asked, amused, as she floundered, trying to look away from him and not succeeding. He moved slowly, watching her eyes fill with him as he cupped her jaw and brought her mouth to his.

The cool, sweet taste tempted, lingered, then slid away before the heat. Her lips moved beneath his, catching, brushing, her breath sweeping across his face.

Then fear moved in her, surging, retreating, shimmering in the shadows. It swirled through the old mill, through the scents of wood and polish. She lay against him, tense and shivering, her fingers digging into his shoulders, her mouth cooled by tears. He kissed them, tasting the salt and rocking her as he would have Keely.

"I don't like people—men—too close to me." Her uneven whisper seemed dragged from her. There was a shudder and a long, painful sigh as she closed her eyes.

When she did not pull away from him, nothing could have kept Quinn from gathering her closer. Quinn fought her withdrawal, the helpless feeling of seeing this strong, fiercely independent, complete woman crawl inside herself.

He acted on instinct, bending to lift her against his chest, carrying her up the stairs to his bedroom. "Quinn..."

"I've never had another woman here. Never wanted one, Tay...." He waited, holding her, while she waded through her emotions. Her fingers lifted, then locked to his shoulders, and Quinn welcomed her trust, gathering her closer.

"Quinn, I'm not up to fighting you now—"

"Shhh..." When she lay on the bed beside him, Quinn eased her head to his shoulder and rocked her. "This is what it's about, Tay. The needing," he whispered, stroking her back. "I need you."

"This is too easy for you. You know how to relate... you've been married...."

He tensed, then said slowly, "I was. Looking back, I see
the need for each other—to care and hold each other—
didn't come into it. Now, here with you, I need to hold you.
You dropped into my life, making the missing parts fit."

"No," she whispered huskily, unevenly, her tone filled
with tears. "I don't want to need anyone."

"Who did this to you?" he asked, smoothing a hand
down her back and noting with satisfaction that she clung
to him.

"I haven't allowed myself to think about it in years." Her
voice was tired, worn, etched with shadows and time. She
sighed, her breath flowing along his cheek. "You upset the
balance in my life, Quinn. I don't like to lose control."

"Do I frighten you?" he asked, his heart missing beats
until she answered.

"You make me angry," she said after a long silence.
"Furious. But no, you don't frighten me."

"Good." He rolled her on top of him, then drew her
mouth down for his kiss. Her lips trembled, warmed and
tasted what he offered. Whatever icy memory she had come
from just now, Quinn wanted to welcome her with gentleness, and every bit of tenderness within him.

"Donovan," she warned, her eyes laughing as she drew
away from him.

Then her hands pushed against his on the pillow. "I don't
want this," she whispered unevenly, lowering her lips to his.
"Not now. Not you."

Her hair spilled around him, filling his senses with the
fresh scent, the silky texture, then the headier scent that was
Taylor's alone. Their fingers linked, his pressed down by
hers, and the arch of her hips thrust against him.

Their eyes met and lingered, slowly, just as their lips had.
Taylor laid her cheek against his, lightly, as though testing
the feel of him against her.

Quinn's heart raged in his chest, and his body ached for
release, yet he sensed that Taylor needed this time, needed
to explore him. Her hands released his, then slid along the
shape of his jaw, his ears.

"Put your hands on me again, Quinn," she whispered after a long, tender kiss.

He eased her breasts into his palms, resenting the light binding of her lingerie and wanting to tear it away. He shook off the need, fearing that she would fly away—that the moment was no more than a lingering wisp of his midnight dreams.

"Donovan," she whispered helplessly, shuddering against him as her hands smoothed his ribs, his lower stomach, and then hovered, floating over the shape of him.

"You've bewitched me...." he whispered unevenly, teasing, fearing her. Wanting her.

Surprise parted her lips, widened her eyes. "Me?"

"Tay, you're driving me crazy. One more touch of those busy fingers and I'll—"

Her hand stroked him over the denim, lightly, gently, curiously, and he nearly leaped from the bed.

Her body tightened against him, shivering, her face pale and tense above him. Quinn forced himself to lay quiet. Shadows of the past clung to her, darkening her eyes until he fell into them. "Tay, were you—?" he asked quietly, sadly, aching for her with his heart, more than with the desire riding his body.

"Taken without my permission?" she supplied flatly. "That's a nice way to put it. Yes, I was." The omission of the dark, ugly word—a woman forced to submit to a man's desire—swirled round the sunlit room, the reflection of the millpond dancing over his bed.

"You're strong now. No one will ever take anything from you again, Tay. Not unless you give it," he soothed, placing his palm over her rapidly beating heart. Taylor closed her eyes, her lashes tipped with sunlight and tears. Then, quietly, slowly, she laid her head against his shoulder and they listened to the water lapping against the still waterwheel.

Taylor stroked his chest, smoothing, then sliding, the hair through her fingers. Quinn held her breast, the sweetness of her body against his too precious to frighten away. "I don't want to think about it," she said huskily, turning her face against his throat and letting the tears come. Then, softly, mournfully, she cried, "Oh, Quinn, there was a baby. I lost a little boy."

He stared at the water's reflection on the coarsely planed boards and damned the pain in Taylor's life. It was then that he discovered tears on his lashes.

Taylor slid away, drawing her life, her pain, with her, moving heavily, as if weighted by chains.

Quinn lay, his arms behind him, staring at the rippling reflection of the millpond on the ceiling, and thought of the woman making her way to Maudie's house. He heard Digger begin barking excitedly and then silence.

Taylor smiled tightly, dusting hands that were now slightly rough from soaps and disinfectants. She'd worked hard, attacking the dust in the house with a vengeance. The lemony scent of furniture polish filled the house, the pots and pans scrubbed and stacked neatly. The old hardwood floors gleamed with wax, the windows clean. She'd washed musty linens and curtains, hanging them to dry in the sunlight and the scent of Maudie's geraniums.

Thoughts of Quinn and Lilian-honey caused her to work harder. As if sensing her mood, Digger had been on his best behavior. He hadn't dug one hole in the rosebushes, though he had managed to tumble a basket of freshly washed clothes to the ground before she could hang them on the line.

She hadn't asked Quinn to hold her tenderly, to rock her in his arms, to listen to her pain. She hadn't asked for anything from him but electricity, telephone hookups and locks—despite the fact that the ladies of Hummingbird Lane had said that locks weren't needed in Blarney.

When Keely's tricycle came creaking to her front door and Digger began to yip, Taylor put aside her dark thoughts of Quinn. She'd given him a piece of her life, and resented the safety of his arms, the sweet, lingering, seductive kisses.

She traveled her life alone, and now here he was, giving her a glimpse of something too dangerous to consider.

One look at him as he worked around the house, and she wanted to slug him. To maul him. He had no right to ripple the waters of her carefully constructed life. To unravel the past. To be so gentle. To admit his need for her. To parade around her doorstep dressed in scraps of torn, paint-spattered jeans and shooting her hot, angry glances.

Taylor pushed freshly cut chamomile, lavender, roses and daisies into a cut-glass vase. It was her right to be angry, not his.

She hadn't asked him to need her.

She didn't want to need him. She didn't want the tenderness he'd offered. Or the passion. Or the laughter.

The thought that Donovan—tough, beguiling, delicious Donovan—had admitted his need to hold her frightened her desperately.

She watched a ladybug crawl to the top of a daisy. She'd always managed quite well, keeping free of attachments, doing her work, and moving on. She touched the daisy, and the ladybug crawled to the top of her finger. Very carefully, Taylor eased aside a curtain and shooed the ladybug away.

When it was time, could she fly away as easily?

She inspected Maudie's house—the neat china ready for tea, the teddy-bear teapot she had sent Maudie from a gift shop in Seattle. When it was time, she would pack them carefully away. She traced the delicate gold pattern on an English bone-china cup. Drinking tea from it at the end of a long, hard day would soothe away stress. Taylor frowned. What was she thinking? She moved quickly, lived out of carry-on flight luggage, and hadn't cared about elegant china, or lacy tablecloths, or getting high on the scent of magnolias and geraniums.

She'd never had a puppy and now she worried about Digger when she left him.

She touched the ladybug's vacated daisy. When it was time, she would pack and leave.

Placing thoughts of Quinn aside as he climbed up the ladder to the roof, his long, tanned legs leading into a tight bottom clad in worn cutoff jeans, was not easy. The sight of his gleaming, corded back and the wind lifting his hair left her drooling. Except at night, when she lay tangled in the sheets on the big brass bed and ached.

Needs? Oh, she had them. But they were better left neatly packed away.

Taylor tossed the surveyor's stakes she'd found on her walk in the garbage and peered out the window. Down by the lake, Quinn lay on a blanket, his arms behind his head, while Keely served tea. The tiny tea service was spread across Quinn's flat, bare stomach, Queenie was perched against his side. When Keely frowned, clearly concerned, Quinn reached out to stroke her black curls.

Taylor had seen Keely's expression before—that of a child dealing with guilt that wasn't rightfully hers.

Taylor jerked back, dragging air into her lungs when she realized she'd stopped breathing. Her heart raced beneath her palm, the fingertips of her other hand clung to the counter for support. "I really don't want this," she said unevenly to the hummingbird hovering in front of the window, staring at her. "I really don't."

Seven

After scratching Digger's long ears, Quinn slammed the screen door to Maudie's back porch behind him. He wanted Taylor to hear him coming. In the five days since she'd shared her past with him, Taylor had lost that haunted look and had taken on a wonderful steamy luster, as if she wanted to take him apart.

He'd decided to take what he wanted, whatever Taylor would spare him. When she was gone, he'd have memories of dimples, hot, smoky eyes, and the soft, loving woman beneath the brittle, impatient screen she used to shield her emotions.

Taylor pleased him, challenged him, brought him back to life. Keely's nightmares had eased for a time, because of Taylor's steady insistence that, though she would go, she would also call and send presents, and come back.

Quinn locked on to the "come back" part. Because when Taylor came back, he'd be waiting. He'd take what he could and hold it until the next time.

He paused long enough to bend his head beneath the sink, letting the cold water cool a bit of his mood. He'd jogged from the mill up the hill to the path leading to the back of Maudie's house—Taylor's house, he corrected, resenting the way he sucked air, winded by a run that had once been easy.

For five days he'd waited at dawn and at dusk for Taylor's yellow running shorts to streak down the hill from Maudie's and return. Little kept him from waylaying her along the way and dragging her into the bushes. He had dreams of tearing away whatever was flattening her chest with his teeth, but he'd decided to give her time to think about their relationship.

She'd frightened him badly when she curled into herself. This morning, before she raised her walls, he intended to have it out with her.

When he straightened from the faucet, water dripping from his hair, a towel hit him in the face. Taylor stood with her hands braced at her waist as he swirled it over his head. Dressed for business in a straight navy blue slack suit, she glared at him over the tortoise-toned frames of small, round glasses perched on her nose. The pencil tucked into the knot on top of her hair quivered with an anger than ran down the length of her willowy body as he dried his bare chest with the towel. Her mouth tightened as she noted his worn, loose running shorts and battered running shoes.

"Won't you join us, Mr. Donovan?" she invited, in a soft tone that made him think of sheathed claws waiting to strike. She jerked the towel from where he had placed it around his neck and slammed it onto the counter.

He bent to kiss the side of her neck, testing the waters, and Taylor inhaled, standing very still. She stepped back, slapped a file against her thigh, then said, "Follow me, please," and led him down the hall to the dining room. She stopped, swept her hand out to indicate the men seated at the dining table. She turned to the seven men. Quinn recognized John Morgan, the accountant type who had drooled over Taylor on their dinner "date," and the backup boys—pretty-boy clones of John, in assorted colorings and heights.

"Gentlemen, this is Mr. Quinn Donovan. He is a local ..."
She dropped the remainder of the sentence, and Quinn
picked his way through "yahoo," "dropout," "beast," and
good old basic "jerk."

The cool dark blue eyes swept over Quinn's bare chest,
paused at the yellow paint running across his left nipple, and
burned a slow path down his tattered jeans. "He may not
look like it now, but Mr. Donovan is a first-rate architect.
I've seen his work. I'd like his input on your plans."

Quinn caught the challenge, the lift of her chin. He could
go or stay. "Gentlemen," he said smoothly, moving past her
into Maudie's dining room. He remembered Taylor's fingers tracing his plans at the mill, her frown of concentration. He studied the elaborate development plans spread
across the table, then helped himself to the plate of small tea
cookies flattening a corner of one of the paper rolls.

Jamison and his hirelings shared a common expression,
which branded Quinn as a "local yokel." He shrugged
mentally, caring little for their opinions. He flipped a cookie
high in the air, and it fell into his mouth. At his side, Taylor inhaled sharply, her expression grim. Quinn crunched
the cookie, fitted a bland expression over his face and wiped
the back of his hand across his mouth. He flicked away the
crumbs.

Taylor's eyes darkened to blue smoke; she steamed perfectly.

He smirked mentally; he was getting to her.

He *wanted* to get to her ... very close to her.

An electronic alarm rang, and from the back porch Digger began to bark frantically. John punched buttons on his
watch, jerking a wary look at Quinn. A beefier man with
jowls and a florid complexion nodded curtly when Taylor
introduced him as Jamison. She introduced the remaining
men, representatives of Randolph Developers, then sat at
the head of the table. Anger flashed in crashing waves from
the beefy man while Taylor coolly flipped through her notes.
"We were just going over the drawings for the condomini-

ums—the vacation and retirement homes—that the Randolph company wants to build on the Culpepper land.''

Digger continued to bark, and Jamison shifted restlessly, the delicate chair creaking beneath his weight. ''Of course, if you want this—Donovan—here, fine. But my experts have already weighed the problems of a development of this nature. You can't expect some backwoods—a resident of this little town to match my team's experience.''

Taylor cut him short with a cool ''Bear with me, please.''

Jamison flicked an impatient, meaningful look at a younger man with a perfect tan and manicure. Quinn studied Junior Number Two's—Marlowe's—white, soft hands and decided that the bones would break very nicely if he touched Taylor. Quinn sat by Taylor, adjusting his height at an angle to hers.

The men stared at him, then at Jamison who pressed his thick lips together. ''Doesn't that dog ever stop barking? Go ahead,'' he snapped, shooting the man named Marlowe another meaningful glance.

Quinn looked at the plans spread on the table. In another minute, the male smorgasbord that Jamison had lined up to sway Taylor would be counting their teeth. When the portrayal of perfect streets, sewage lagoons, tennis courts, golf courses and sprawling condominiums wound down, Quinn yawned and stretched, concealing the need to toss the lot of them out Maudie's front door. In Quinn's experience, Jamison was cut from the breed of developer who would cut corners for profit, leaving a mess in his wake.

A few years ago, Quinn had broken the nose of a man just like Jamison. For good reason. It had been worth the beating he took from hired goons later.

He stretched again, denying the tightening in his stomach caused by his quick surge of anger. Taylor stiffened at his side, straightening in her chair. Her pencil paused in its exact, blocky printing. He caught her quick, stealthy glance down his body before she studied the notes scrawled on the file.

Because she looked so precise, so perfect and cool, Quinn
eased his jogger beneath her business pump. He lifted and
bobbed it slightly. She frowned, then flipped open the file
on the table in front of her. Quinn recognized it as the information he'd compiled and given to Moriarity. "According to my sources, this community thrives because of the
lake. The natural springwater is bottled, the profits shared
by the town and invested in community-owned financial
plans. The gristmill is a historical site in Blarney and should
be preserved. Mr. Donovan has completely renovated the
millhouse. There is a rich heritage here, gentlemen. It should
be treated gently."

Quinn bobbed his toe, lifting her foot, as he thought
about how he wanted to treat her, gently or matching the
passion within her. He inhaled the subtle, cool scents, sorting them—soap, shampoo, then something deeper, a feminine essence he would recognize all his life.

Taylor's heel bored into Quinn's toe, and she smiled at
him briefly, smugly.

"So? He's a carpenter. We'll find him a job on the con-
struction crews," Jamison muttered, then inhaled impatiently when Taylor slashed him a cool look.

"He's an excellent architect. If I may continue... The
lake's ecology is delicate, based on the tiny shad. Oil, ce-
ment or other unnatural materials in the water could destroy them. A heavy rainfall could take chemicals directly
into the lake. So you see why I am considering all facets of
your offer."

Jamison nodded. "If the fish need something special to
live, we'll get the fish whatever food they need. They say the
bass fishing is great here. That will bring in the sportsmen.
Morrison, tap those keys a little harder. Let's see if we can
up the dollars for this property and make this little lady
happy, so we can all go about our business. I know she has
a job to get back to, just like we do."

Taylor's hands went flat on the table, then flexed just
once, very slowly. "Dollars won't cut it."

Jamison snorted in disbelief. Taylor swung her eyes to Quinn, the cold fury in her eyes concealed, her smile tight. "What do you think, Mr. Donovan?"

He thought that John and Marlowe were very experienced with women. That Jamison had brought them along to serve up to Taylor as dessert. Taylor's foot pressed down on his, her eyes narrowing, prompting him. "No way," he said flatly, answering her question. "The angle of the hill is too steep. The soil is shallow there, with layers of rock that would have to be blasted. Any change to the face of the hills surrounding the lake will destroy it. Removal of trees and underbrush will cause what soil there is to wash off straight into the lake."

"Hell, man. Of course the hills have to be cleared and bulldozed. Maybe just a little blasting. People want a view of the lake. Serenity and all that," Jamison shot back in disgust. "This town can use the progress. Why doesn't someone go shut that dog up?"

"He's my dog and he's in my home. He's just fine. This meeting is concluded, Mr. Jamison. I have decided not to sell at this time."

"I thought you were starting to be reasonable. You're making a big mistake. Think of the employment, the job opportunities for the locals."

Taylor smiled tightly and stood. "Employment was one of my considerations. I had hoped for a different discussion of our priorities, Mr. Jamison. As I said, money isn't everything. This community is unique. I want to see it stay that way. Good day, gentlemen."

Jamison lumbered to his feet, slashing a contemptuous look at Quinn. "I'll bet the locals butter your backside," he said with a sneer. Then his tone shifted to menacing. "You'll sell, little lady, mark my words. We know this land can be made to pay out, that the investment will be good for us. So all we have to do is to reach the right price."

No one was buttering Taylor's backside but himself, Quinn decided, and began to rise to his feet. For that matter no one would imply that anyone else had the right to butter her backside but him. And no one would threaten her.

Her light touch on his shoulder and her meaningful glance tethered him. Her face was too pale, the only outward sign of her tight control. She braced her hands on the table, studied them and said quietly, "I run a major corporation, Mr. Jamison. If you want problems so deep, so wide, that your plans will never find a site anywhere, *ever*, then by all means take me on."

When Quinn stood slowly, wondering how he could toss the men outside without damaging the furniture, Taylor shot him a warning look. Jamison stepped forward, his jowls quivering.

Quinn doubted that Jamison's pretty boys had ever been in a country brawl. Maybe it was time they had the experience. He smiled tightly, nastily. "Gentlemen?" he invited softly.

Taylor glanced up at him, frowned and stepped in front of him. She pushed her shoulder back against his chest, and Quinn sensed that she was protecting him. Guarding him. Stunned, he mulled the idea as her elbow jabbed him in the stomach. She inhaled and walked to the door, opening it, then hesitated.

Quinn glanced out into the street and found Moriarity tucking tickets on the windshields of two long custom limousines. The fines would be stiff for out-of-towners. Higher because the limousines were black and Moriarity reasoned that only criminals preferred black to silver limousines. A narrow-thinking man, Quinn's cousin had been pleased that Taylor's rental car was gray. Taylor's left cheek dimpled slightly before she said, "Good day, gentlemen. As I said, our business is finished. And for your information, I love my dog's barking. Donovan . . . stay."

She watched the two limousines glide down the hill, then locked the door. She turned to Quinn, her arms crossed over her chest. "I cannot say that I have ever played footsie during a business meeting," she said very precisely between her teeth. "I thought we had an agreement—though we haven't ashed out the rules. You have been staying in your life, and have been staying in mine. I like it that way. Now, why are ou here?'' Bristling with anger, she stalked toward him.

"You are a passionate woman, Tay," he murmured, meaning it.

"Passionate? I'll show you passionate like you've never een before. I am angry, very angry, with you. In fact I have a reputation for never losing my temper. You are causing xceptions all over the place. What are you doing in my house, Donovan? Do you realize what those men thought when they left here?''

She tossed the pencil she'd been tapping on her palm to he table. The natural-silk business jacket over her breasts ifted once as she held her breath, then she exploded elegantly. "I'll tell you what they think—that you walk in here very day, dip that fine head of hair beneath my kitchen faucet to cool off, then shuck those well-stuffed shorts and..."

She hesitated, blinked, and a blush began moving up from her throat. She swallowed again while Quinn watched, amused. Her eyes widened as he reached to smooth her hot cheek. "Well-stuffed?" he prodded, entranced, as Taylor's hand fluttered to her throat.

She cleared her throat, backing away slightly, her eyes wary. "Quinn. You must know that we do not react well to each other," she said, very precisely. "Now, as long as you realize that I will do the best in my power for Blarney Flats, perhaps you can...um..."

"You'll always do your best, Tay...because you're sweet and good, and very, very soft."

"Soft? Me?"

"Very soft." Quinn extracted the pencil thrust into the ight topknot of hair, and a curl followed it. He toyed with it, placing one hand on the wall beside her. The pulse running along her throat throbbed heavily, and he kissed it, fitting his lips over the beat, then tasting that warm skin with he tip of his tongue.

Taylor inhaled sharply and straightened her shoulders a
if preparing to fight. "Look, Quinn, there's no need to play
this game any further. I've never done business that way."

He nuzzled her temple, entranced by the shiver that se
duced and beckoned. This was what he'd needed, what drew
him running toward her house after five long, hungry
days—the softness and the scent and the passion lurking
beneath her cool shield. "Mmm? Game? Business?"

"I'm aware of how much this community means to you
That you would...ah...want to sway anyone holding the
title to the Culpepper lands."

Her hair unfurled slowly, sliding silkily along his cheek
No one could raise his emotions faster than this woman, he
realized when she moved restlessly, easing away from him
He placed his hands on her waist and jerked her back
against him hard. "Don't put it in words, Tay. Just don't,"
he warned between his teeth, grinding the back ones. "Are
you frightened of me? Of being close to me?"

Her brows jerked into a frown. "Of course not."

"Good," he stated flatly, meaning it. "So, tucked up
here, left alone in your nice safe castle, you've decided
what?" he prodded.

The wary flicker of her eyes preceded an uneven "Quinn
please don't embarrass both of us." He lifted an eyebrow a
that, realizing that with very little effort from her he could
embarrass himself quite nicely. "I'll do the best I can for the
community, though it may take time. You've made it clear
that you don't want..." Her sentence dropped off as she
tried to ease around him.

"'Don't want?'" Quinn jerked her back, his hands low
on her hips. He eased her against him, insinuating one leg
between her soft ones. He nudged her gently before he
cupped her bottom and lifted her slowly up to eye level with
him.

"You know, Donovan. This is an awkward position," she
stated unevenly as he tugged open the top button to her suit
with his teeth.

"You could wrap your legs around my waist," Quinn offered bluntly, then closed his eyes as he thought about those legs.

"You're shuddering, Donovan. You look so...so hot and desperate.... Maybe you had better run more cold water over your head," Taylor said in a thread of a whisper. She blew a curl away from her cheek. Another curl tumbled over her shoulder, then swirled around the navy cloth covering the tip of her breast, and Quinn's mouth went dry.

"Digger has stopped barking," he noted absently. He lifted her higher, burying his face in her breasts, kissing the softness. He brought her closer, nuzzling aside the material. He stopped, wrapped in her scents and the knowledge that she wore nothing beneath her suit jacket. He double-checked his find with another brief nuzzle. "Tay. *You are not wearing underwear.*"

She hesitated, uncertain with their intimacy. She'd never shared her life before, but Quinn seemed so incensed, so stunned, that she offered him an explanation. "I...I've been sensitized lately, and I wanted to concentrate on the business meeting."

"Sensitized? Hell, *I'm* sensitized," Quinn muttered darkly and wondered how he could manage to get her all the way to the bedroom.

"You're shaking, Quinn," she reminded him delicately, precisely. She inhaled sharply when he buried his face in her throat, diving into her intimate scents. "Perhaps you should put me down."

He closed his eyes and forced his thumbs to stop stroking her hips. He wanted every question settled between them. "The Culpepper estate has nothing to do with us, Tay," he said firmly, concealing the raging storm inside him.

Her fingertips began to stroke his shoulder, toying with the ends of his hair, drifting along his jawbone. She touched the corner of his lips delicately. "You're so beautiful. Especially when you're in a macho snit," she whispered unevenly, studying his face, her fingertips quivering on his skin, floating quickly over his shoulders, his arms.

Quinn tried to breathe, fascinated by Taylor's dimple. "You know you are," she whispered, teasing him, smoothing his chest, spearing her pale fingers through the dark hair, tugging it gently. "You're magnificent. So stop looking as if I've insulted you."

"Magnificent." He snorted in disbelief, broadsided by her delight and his embarrassment. He snorted again, dismayed by the heat running across his cheekbones.

Wary of her now, Quinn eased her to her feet. "Hart, you're a witch," he managed when he could. "And I'm not a pretty boy. The thought is disgusting..." he uttered roughly, because she had bent to tease his nipple with her teeth.

When she flicked the hard nub with her tongue and grinned cockily, Quinn grabbed the front of the waistband of her slacks in his fist. He jerked her to him. "Tell me one more time that I don't frighten you," he demanded, his heart pounding.

Her head went back, her eyes stormy with disdain. "No. You don't frighten me. Not for a minute. I can take you on anytime, Donovan."

"We'll see," he said grimly, bending to scoop her up into his arms. She shrieked elegantly, indignantly. "Oh, great. This is the macho big-strong-man scene where you carry me up the stairs. Once was enough, thank you." But pleasure ran through her tone, and Quinn counted on delighting her even more.

Her eyes widened as he leered, lifting his eyebrows twice. "You wouldn't. Donovan, put me down. You'll hurt yourself." Quinn snorted, thinking of what was hurting and what would cure it.

"You'll hurt yourself," she repeated darkly, crossing her arms over her chest and settling in for the ride. "Don't sue me for your hospital bill. This is all your idea, Donovan," she continued as he swept up the stairs.

At the next to the last step she stopped talking and cautiously placed her head on his shoulder. He hesitated when her lips brushed his throat. Her hands held him now, tightly.

"Donovan, since you seem so grim, so determined for this event..."

Against his throat, her face warmed. "...I want you to know this isn't an everyday occurrence for me."

He tossed her lightly on the bed, then stood back, slowly taking in the view. Distracted by the length and curve of her legs, by the shifting of breasts he knew were free now, he murmured, "Tay, this isn't a common event for me, either. I haven't been with a woman since Keely's conception."

"I thought men..." She sighed, her eyes widening as he eased his shorts away.

Fearing that she would turn him away now, he sucked in air and held it. Quinn's hands curled into fists; he'd lost the clean lines of his boyhood, hair matted his chest, damp with sweat in the bedroom's sweet, still air. *Would she leave him now?* Heavy with desire, his heart lurched as she sought the shadows of his stomach and lower. He balled his hands into fists, fighting for control and crushing the tiny, intimate packet he'd taken from his running shorts. If she walked out now, he'd live...just barely.

When Taylor closed her eyes and shuddered, his heart stopped. "Yes," she whispered slowly, firmly, in the shadowy, still heat. "Perhaps we should," she added, in the very precise way she used when her passions ran deep.

In the center of the huge bed, she seemed too vulnerable. The knuckles of her hands shone whitely, her fists grabbing the quilt. "Tay?" he whispered hoarsely, his body hurting.

Yet he could wait for her. Wait until forever.

Time seemed to stop. On the bureau, the small fan sweeping promises and scents around the room rotated from side to side. Leaves shifted in the bright sunlight beyond the room, stirred by the slight rose-scented breeze. Her hummingbird paused on the way to his feeder, hovering, staring at her before zipping away.

She tossed back her hair, rising from the bed to unbutton her jacket. She turned away from him, undressing slowly. He swallowed, the need to take her storming through him. Yet he gave her this moment to choose.

Taylor's fingers trembled as she slid the jacket's buttons from their holes one by one, as if she were making cautious, sound decisions that would last her lifetime. She wanted to come to him on her terms, not his alone. She folded the jacket and placed it over the top of a chair, then her slacks pooled to the floor. Behind her, Quinn inhaled sharply, then groaned deep in his chest.

"You sat in that room downstairs, doing business in a room filled with men, wearing only *those?*" He sounded incensed, outraged, his scowl fierce.

She decided to keep the thigh-high stockings in place for the time, and turned to him. "My suit was lined, thank you very much," she said primly, fighting the urge to jerk her clothing in front of her as Quinn's eyes moved over her slowly, hungrily. His gaze paused at her breasts, and Taylor fought the wild shiver running through her before Quinn's inspection lowered.

A curtain fluttered at the open window, brushing her bare hip, and Taylor jumped slightly.

Quinn's hot stare jerked to her breasts. "Come here." There was nothing easy or gentle about his low tone.

Taylor lifted her head, determined to meet him on her own terms. He looked so arrogant, so challengingly male, and so untamed, yet a strong tide of gentleness ran beneath the surface. He gave her every choice, his eyes willing her to come to him, to choose what would happen between them.

She decided—while her mouth dried and her breasts tingled, and funny little zings melted her thighs—that she would just keep her stockings where they were. It was a small, safe decision. Because she had already decided, taking in the taut line of Quinn's hard body, that she wanted him.

With an impatient groan, Quinn ripped away the hand-sewn quilt, tossing it over the rocker.

The dark shadows of his body caught her—the hollow of a hip, the ripple of corded muscle across his chest as he turned back the sheet. He tensed, and both nipples jumped on the pads of muscle beneath them. The second time the dark nubs bounced within their hairy nest, her mouth dried again and her stomach lurched, following the ripples downward.

Then he was lifting her, holding her against him as they tumbled into bed.

Quinn's eyes were gentle as he held her against him, stroking her. They fit neatly together, curve against angle, smooth against rough. "The bed creaks," she whispered, the heat of his body swirling into her. "Digger will bark."

He chuckled outright, and she grinned, launching herself on top of him.

Then the room stilled as he lay beneath her. Quinn's hands smoothed her back, her hips, running down her thighs and back up to carefully fit over her breasts. "Come here, Tay," he whispered unevenly, longingly, while his rough hands gently caressed and molded her.

His lips coaxed hers open, enticing her tongue to prowl in the mysterious depths. Quinn's fullness warmed her stomach, challenging her, enticing her. He let her set the pace as she dived into the scent of him, easing closer to the hard, shifting roughness beneath her. He groaned, cupping the back of her head to deepen the kiss, his finger and thumb smoothing the tip of her breast. Her legs moved, shifting restlessly, settling beside his thighs.

Beneath her, Quinn shuddered, his hands trembling. He lifted and gently eased her down on him.

Filled slowly, gently, by him, her hands digging into the safety of his solid shoulders, Taylor fought for control.

She lost. Heat spiraled through her, the fit complete. Then Quinn's mouth trailed down her throat to take her breast.

At the first tug of his lips, she was soaring, straining against him, filling, bursting. She tightened, rippled, took him greedily, before the pleasure could fly away.

"Tay?" Quinn murmured, a heartbeat or a lifetime later. Trembling, he gathered her closer, his breathing rough against her throat. His body tensed, throbbing, still filling her.

When she could breathe, Taylor managed unevenly, helplessly, "I can't move."

"Good. Don't," he said tightly, holding very still.

"You are very tense, Quinn," she whispered warily.

"Yes, that I am," he admitted, miming her very precise speech. "You are doing very well, Tay. Keep movement to a minimum, please. I believe we can continue proceedings in a minute." His smile moved along her cheek, his teeth tugged at her earlobe.

He caressed her breast, murmuring soft, gentle words while the heat storming within her settled slightly. She turned to him, smoothing his cheek and allowing her fingers to be suckled one by one. She had never played, and with Quinn, now in this safe, summer-scented room, she wanted everything.

Their eyes met and locked, then Quinn's large, rough hands eased her knees upward, so that she crouched over him, deepening their intimacy.

When the second rippling began, the delight widening Taylor's eyes, Quinn strained with her, arcing his body up to hers.

Taylor blew away the curl that tickled her cheek. She didn't want to open her eyes.

She knew she couldn't move. Her bones had melted. Tiny little hot ping-pings continued to quiver within her.

"Tay..." Quinn whispered close to her ear, his voice raspy and deep, laced with laughter.

She was dreaming again, tangled in her sheets. She jerked the sheet, trying to free it, and found a hair-roughened, muscular thigh.

Her lids opened, and Quinn leaned over her, grinning roguishly, smugly. While she lay under the sheet, he lay over it.

Quinn's large hand smoothed her breast, cupping it lazily. "Keely will be home soon ... I've got to go, Tay. Wake up and kiss me goodbye."

She blinked owlishly, trying to find her bearings. The bedside clock read three; the afternoon sun heated the room.

Quinn's long hard body lay beside hers. He smelled of soap, and his hair damp against her throat.

She inhaled, closed her eyes and said slowly, "We have just...just...in the middle of the day..." She checked the bedside clock again and groaned.

His grin widened as he traced her flush. "Just...?"

"You know... The bed creaked, and Digger barked...." He was grinning now, teasing her. People did not tease Winscott's "Steel Hart." She tried the notion on, weighing whether she liked Quinn teasing her or not.

Winscott's "Steel Hart" tried to move—and couldn't.

She had pooled into a warm, oozy, happy smile all down her body. She let the smile slide back up to her lips and found that they tasted of his hunger.

Lying this close to Quinn didn't clarify her thinking processes. Her body was slightly sore, tingling, and wanting to replay whatever sensations had disintegrated her—she rechecked the bedside clock—over an hour ago.

Disintegrated. Yes. That was the correct word. Whatever had happened with Quinn had set off fiery explosions that rippled and totally shattered her into a hundred little perfect golden clouds. She remembered floating gently down into his arms. While she had lain, unable to move, draped over his damp, safe body, Quinn had continued the long quieting strokes of his hands on her back, the gentle whispers, the tender reassuring kisses on her teary lashes.

"Give me a kiss, Tay, to carry me through," he whispered, nibbling at her lips, tugging the bottom one with his teeth. "Keely will be coming home from Mother's, and Moriarity is picking up his wife's table. If I..." He swallowed, his gaze sweeping down her body. "There will be gossip if I stay. Come to the mill later. Stay the night."

She trembled, unable to step into his world just yet.

"I'll call you later," he pressed, drawing her hand to his mouth.

Quinn's meadow green eyes were tender, tracing her slightly swollen lips. "I've drawn your bath, Tay. Soaking will help..." Then he frowned, smoothing the sheet over her stomach, spanning it with his hand. "Did I hurt you?" he asked impatiently, rawly, the line between his brows deepening.

She placed her hands over his. While he had acted outrageously with Jamison's crew, he had touched her exquisitely, his big, rough hands trembling. "No."

"I don't want to leave you alone now."

She thought of another man, years before, roughly shoving away a young girl when he was finished.

For her answer, she gave him the kiss he'd wanted, letting him know she understood. The kiss was long and sweet and promising and laced with hunger. When he stood, moving reluctantly away, she ached, alone in the shadows of the sunlit room.

At eleven o'clock that night, Quinn held Keely's sleeping body against him, rocking her as he watched the light in Taylor's bedroom up on Hummingbird Lane. Keely's nightmare had immediately followed his telephone call to Taylor.

He shouldn't have pushed her.

Her tone had been brisk, noncommittal, enraging him. She'd spoken precisely, nettling him, and keeping up the walls. No, it wasn't possible for her to visit him later that night. As far as he could tell, she had taken the magical, sweet passion, placed it in a neat capsule and put it aside on a shelf. She'd meandered through a listing of possibilities for the land and dismissed him with a disconnecting buzz of the telephone.

Quinn had wanted to rip his telephone from the wall and carry it to her.

What had he expected?

More. In his fancies and "druthers," his body hungering for more, Quinn had expected her to come to him. To lie in the loft with him the whole night, while Keely slept safely in her bed.

Quinn smoothed Keely's back as she gave a last deep, shuddering sigh. Keely had cried, certain that her mother had gone to heaven because of her.

His daughter had wanted her. Despite his pride, Quinn was just desperate enough, as Keely had sobbed, to take her to Taylor. Then, suddenly, his daughter slept, exhausted by her day.

Quinn rammed his fingers through his hair for the twentieth time. When he closed his eyes, the memory of Taylor's discovery, her pleasure, curled around him.

He frowned and continued to stroke Keely's small, vulnerable back, nuzzling her jumbled curls.

Out in the night, Sir Elmo bellowed and the tree frogs chorused. Quinn had seen Taylor in action—cool, cutting, maneuvering Jamison's men out her front door, dropping the matter of the land purchase.

He refused to be maneuvered. Or dropped. But he'd made a mistake with Taylor that he wouldn't make again.

"Our Tay has a fight on her hands, Keely," he whispered, acknowledging that only his four-year-old daughter kept him from Taylor that night. "She's dissecting what happened right now, planning to stuff it away."

Quinn resented her entering his life, stirring the restless needs within him. He'd stored them away carefully, and now he needed her desperately.

After two cold showers, and fitful dreams of Taylor's pale body, the long, gently curved legs, clad in thigh-high stockings, gliding toward him, Quinn finally slept at dawn.

Eight

The following afternoon, Taylor settled back in a chair of the Blarney Pub, easing her jean-clad legs beneath a scarred table.

Intimate tingles, reminding her of Quinn's lovemaking, began when she shifted.

She'd made love to Quinn within three weeks of meeting him. Winscott's "Steel Hart" always planned her events, scheduled her time and weighed opportunities. She balanced and weighed decisions calmly.

Making love with Quinn had been her decision. She took the responsibility.

He'd seemed so solid, yet so vulnerable, standing in her frilly, feminine bedroom.

She ran her finger along the damp rim of the beer mug in front of her. She'd forever remember the sight of his black hair spreading across the lace-trimmed pillow shams.

She shrugged, smoothing the lace at her wrists. The old-fashioned blouse, with romantic, billowy sleeves tucked into a tight cuff suited the jeans and the pub perfectly. The high collar and its lace also served to cover the small reddened patches left by Quinn's rough cheek. She flushed, thinking of the small marks on her breasts, and studied her new red cowboy boots.

Quinn's tone on the telephone had been curt, demanding, and had left her very little room to think. Her uncertain emotions had snarled back.

Taylor straightened her shoulders and adjusted the lace around her thoat. She wasn't here at this hour to think of Quinn, though thoughts of him kept popping into her brain at the strangest times. Used to controlling her moods, her thoughts, Taylor pressed her lips together. She methodically picked through ways of adding red as accessories to her basic navy, gray and black business wardrobe, then swung her thoughts to her plans for the day. Schedules had to be met, and the men-only hour—or rather two hours, if they counted correctly—was on her upcoming-events schedule.

The memorable lovemaking with Quinn, and the resulting emotional upheaval, were not going to delay this reckoning. The men of Blarney Flats would be sharing their notorious "hour" with one Taylor Hart.

All in all, she felt wonderful. In control and very happy. Tip-top shape. The baby Loch Ness and his shad were safe. Digger adored her as much as she loved him. Her morning run trimmed off the excess energy she'd experienced throughout the night. Keely had given her a genuine four-leaf clover to entrap her own leprechaun. Taylor grinned. Yes! She was definitely up to the challenge of the Blarney Pub.

She surveyed the gathering crowd of men, who glanced anxiously at her as the clock neared three. With ten minutes to go until the men-only hour, she noted that the men here now were older, possibly retired. She studied the pub's dark beer in front of her, the thick layer of foam. Still, retired or not, the men shouldn't exclude women.

Taylor hoped her hair would remain in its tight knot. She wanted to look cool and effective. She allowed herself a small, amused smile. Taylor Hart, newly entered into pub executive status, dressed for...Arkansas pubbing.

A muscular man with thick gray hair and rugged features that reminded her of Quinn entered the room. Heavier and shorter than Quinn, he surveyed the shadows and found her instantly. She thought she noted a bit of Quinn's swagger as the man ordered a beer and carried it to her table.

"It's time we met. I'm James Donovan, Molly's husband. Quinn and Cadell are my boys, Keely is my granddaughter." His voice softened, almost musically, reminding her of Cade's. "Then there's our daughter, Briana Marie," James continued, looking at her closely.

"Hello. I'm—"

"My granddaughter's famous Tay... Taylor Hart, Maudie's great-niece," he supplied. "May I sit down?"

Taylor liked him immediately. "Certainly."

"So you're the one who has Quinn snarling," he said thoughtfully, easing into a chair. "I can see why."

She wondered distantly what the record number of blushes was for one day. She'd experienced her lifetime quota on her morning run, and hoped the townspeople would think her flushed coloring was the result of her exercise. "I've met Quinn," she said, very precisely. "He's painting Maudie's house and refinishing her furniture. I've decided to keep it."

"He's good at painting and refinishing," James said slowly, his eyes twinkling. "Apparently the men think he's good at keeping you on the straight and narrow, because they've just sent for him. It's fallen to him to oust you out of here."

"Fine," she said tightly, not ready to face Quinn just yet. "Let him try."

"You're good for Keely... Quinn, too," James said slowly, watching the clock. "Two minutes until three."

She smiled sweetly at Blarney's best, the men standing uncertainly around the bar. "What do they do in here for two hours?"

James shrugged, turning his beer in his big, rough, squarish hands to study the foam. "It's the local spit-and-whittlers. Mostly retired gents, shooed away from under their wives' feet. Once in a while a farmer or two drops in to visit before going on his way. With Cadell doing the ranching now, I drop in a couple times a week when Molly sends me on errands."

"They don't need to be frightened of me."

James raised his eyebrows as Quinn sauntered through the door, dressed in a rag of a T-shirt, jeans with holes and scruffed boots. His hair curled at his broad shoulders as he stood in the doorway, looking like a gunslinger ready for a showdown.

James tipped back on the legs of his chair. He folded his hands over his stomach and rocked leisurely as he watched his son approach. "Afternoon, Quinn Daniel. Just dropping by?"

"Dad." Quinn's eyes raked Taylor's. "Out," he ordered her flatly, indicating the door with a jerk of his head. Sawdust fluttered from his hair to his shoulders.

Taylor smiled tightly, incensed by his tone. No one had ever spoken to her in that curt, dark snarl. He was angry from the night before, when he'd called to demand her presence. Well, she'd wanted space from him then—and she wanted it now. To settle her nerves, she picked up the cold mug and drank a good third of its contents before saying very clearly, "I do not think I am ready to go just yet."

"Women!" a man snorted at the bar.

James continued to rock on the back legs of his chair, looking with interest from his son to Taylor and back again. While Quinn loomed over them, Taylor drank another third of the dark beer. Quinn and James looked at each other. "Have a seat, Quinn Daniel," James offered. "This could take a while."

"You know, James, your son is a bully. No offense to you or Molly or Cade or Briana," she added carefully.

"True. Quinn has always wanted his way, no ifs or buts. Few things have kept him from his course, once he's set his mind." James nodded as Quinn sprawled into a chair.

Taylor glanced at the hole in his shirt, then at the clock. "I have a perfect right to be here."

James nodded. "True."

"That beer is home brew. It's going to knock you on your high-class, fine-looking butt," Quinn stated flatly.

"Is that any way to speak to the girl?" James asked, humor lacing his tone.

"No way at all. One should refer to that specific part of a woman's anatomy as a derriere, if at all," Taylor stated precisely because her head had started getting very light. "I hope he doesn't talk to his sister like that."

James chuckled. "Bria can hold her own with Cadell and Quinn."

Quinn's lips curved. Someone from the bar yelled, "She can outrun you, Donovan. I'll mow the city hall lawn for a month if she can't."

Taylor sniffed delicately. She was trying not to be obvious as she watched the hole on Quinn's tattered T-shirt. It framed his nipple. He moved, and the dark nub jumped, delighting her. Lord, she loved his chest. "...and tush," she added aloud very primly. Then she said to Blarney's best— to the men at the bar: "Of course I can outrun Donovan. He was out of breath when he ran up the hill to my house yesterday morning."

One man cleared his throat. The only sound in the echoing silence.

The lines beside Quinn's eyes deepened. His father chuckled. Taylor loved the rich, rolling sound. She grinned at him widely, liking him very much.

"Tay, you're putting your class-A derriere in a sling," Quinn murmured.

While she stared at the nipple that had jumped within the hole of his shirt, a man at the bar growled, "A Flynn is alvays faster than a Donovan. I say the woman has Flynn blood in her.''

Taylor frowned, her mouth drying as she thought about Quinn lying beneath her. "How do you do that?" she asked breathlessly, fascinated, as he crossed his arms.

"What?"

"That nipple-jump thing."

James guffawed outright, spewing his last sip of beer aside on the floor.

Quinn inhaled, his chest tightened, the nipple jumped, and a red stain slid across his cheekbones. "You did it again," Taylor exclaimed delightedly.

From the bar, one man snarled, "I say Flynns can out-run Donovans any day." Then: "The woman isn't a Flynn or a Donovan, so she doesn't count."

"I say the girl has Flynn blood," Edward Flynn tossed into the heated exchange.

"Get out, while the going is good, Tay," Quinn warned lightly, experienced with the families' feuding. In another moment, Joshua Flynn would be tossing his mug at the mirror, which had been replaced hundreds of times in one hundred and twenty or so years. Eighty-five-year-old Orion Donovan would be boasting about how he—as a fifteen-year-old "boyo"—had broken the noses of two Flynns in a brawl. The brawls were verbal now, but with Taylor tossing her equal rights at the men's feet, anything could happen. "Get out now, or I will remove you."

Because she was absolutely certain Quinn was not ordering Winscott's top lady CEO to do anything, Taylor pushed back her chair and lifted her mug in a toast. "Here's to Quinn Daniel Donovan. May he eat my dust."

Three hours later, at a quarter of seven, Quinn rang Maudie's doorbell. Coming from inside the house, Chuck Berry's loud, hot rock and roll guitar music clashed with the gentle summer night.

While Digger barked excitedly, Quinn stared at the flowers in his hand, the sharp crease in his only pair of good jeans and the new shine on his boots. He inhaled the magnolia scents of Hummingbird Lane, noted the huge, waxy white flowers gleaming in the sunset. Taylor had taken an early run—he knew that because he was watching her when he scorched his shirt. She should have showered by now. The thought of her taking a shower, or the bath he had drawn yesterday afternoon, dried Quinn's throat.

What was he doing on Taylor's doorstep?

He didn't have a thing Taylor might want. Not a thing to offer her. She'd be leaving in a week. Soaring out of Blarney Flats and leaving him aching.

Quinn shifted restlessly. If he had any sense, he'd let her cool down a bit before pushing her. He frowned. Taylor was not a woman to be pushed into anything.

What the hell was he doing here?

Taking what he could get, he answered.

Quinn glanced at his battered heavy-duty pickup, which was parked in front of the millhouse. John's sleek gray sports car fit Taylor better. Quinn gritted his teeth, muttered where and what Junior could do and where, and jammed the doorbell twice, impatiently. Chuck Berry's music stopped, and Taylor jerked open the door. She looked up at him through the screen door. "Go away. The race for Saturday is on. Three days from now. Seven point two miles, from the city park. Up to the Scotsman's grave to pick a shamrock and back. You can't change my mind, so don't try."

She paused, flipped on the overhead porch light and peered through the screen door to take in his white dress shirt, pressed jeans and shined boots. He took in her hot pink bodysuit, the sweat darkening the area between her breasts and the damp curls clinging to her hot cheeks. "Go away," she said again, closing the door.

Digger whined when Quinn opened the screen door. He inserted his spit-polished boot toe into the closing door, pushed it open gently with one hand and thrust the flowers at her. She sniffed them appreciatively, stroked his mother's best red roses and jerked them away from him. Over the bouquet, Taylor said tightly, "I did not have a 'buzz on' at the pub, as you accused me of, Donovan. I knew what I was doing when I challenged you. You're entirely too arrogant, and it's time someone took you down a notch. That someone is me." She looked at his boot meaningfully.

He eased his neck to one side, regretting the nervous impulse to use iron-on starch on his collar. He also regretted tugging Taylor down to his lap after her challenge and kissing her. He hadn't intended to, but at that moment he'd felt young and flat-out good. She had been stunned, scrambling out of his lap and steaming out of the pub.

"If we're having an affair, Tay," he stated, warily but firmly, "you'll have to bend a bit."

The flowers quivered in her hand. Her eyebrows lifted to the damp headband. The mound of curls perched on top of her head trembled. "Affair?" she asked, in a tense, uneven voice that Quinn found very sexy.

He placed his hand on the door, opening it slightly, despite her protesting grip. "When two people make love... when they make commitments that they haven't made to other people... That's what we did, Tay darlin'. We made commitments and love."

Quinn omitted that they'd made love too quickly. There had been no time for the gentleness that he wanted to show her, before or after. The instant fusion between them had knocked aside his control.

What control? Taylor had collapsed in a beautiful, delightful, ego-building, limp, damp sprawl across him.

"Oh...was that what it was?" she asked archly. "I do not have affairs. Once does not an affair make, Donovan. I'm certain things like that happen every day." She paused, meeting his frown. "Okay, Quinn. I *know* people make love every day. But not me. I have to deal with this carefully. In the best way I know, and that is to stay cool—which I can't seem to do with you nearby, *because you're either picking me up or pulling me into your lap*—and balance out what has passed in these three weeks and how to deal with it... with you." She had exploded softly during the "picking me up" part, but she managed to get her voice down to a very precise, cool tone later.

"Tay..." he warned, then watched the angle of her jaw tighten. He clamped down a list of arguments about why they had made love. He tried again. "Would you like to go for a walk with me?" If he could just get her by the lake, it was just a short walk to the millhouse and his bed.

It was very important to him that Taylor share his bed. He hadn't had another woman in his millhouse bedroom. He wasn't used to sharing Keely, or his life. Of course, he was likely to make errors, he told himself.

Damn it. He hadn't wanted a woman as badly as he wanted Taylor. He had geared himself to raise Keely safely. He hadn't thought beyond that.

Pulling Taylor down on his lap had been an impulse brought on by a dose of sheer happiness. She'd had him off balance, blinding him with dimples and that victorious cocky grin. The lacy, old-fashioned blouse had started him thinking of her nightgown, of the frilly pillows on her bed. The tight, leggy jeans had reminded him of Taylor's pale body clad only in those thigh-high stockings as she walked toward him, her eyes dark and mysterious. His instincts at the pub had told him to hold her close, to cuddle her. She'd landed beautifully in his lap, and his body had reacted immediately.

Quinn frowned. Treating Taylor by instinct had proven to be a mistake.

He'd hoped that the bouquet of flowers would boost his chances of finding himself snuggled next to Taylor at dawn. Hell, it wasn't every day that he sweated an entire hour over an ironing board, pressing and scorching whatever jeans and shirts he could find. He thought of the high stack of ruined clothes by his ironing board.

He reached behind him to tuck the scorch mark inside his waistband and hoped the magnolia and honeysuckle scents of the night would cover the smell of burned cloth. Discussing Keely's day, ironing, waiting for Taylor's run, planning how to apologize, all at the same time, wasn't easy.

When she ran early, her expression dark and furious, he'd watched her, gauged his possibilities and scorched his shirt.

From that moment his day had worsened: the stain on Keely's best ruffled pink polka-dot sunsuit had to be soaked and Queenie had gotten lost and Moriarity had turned up for his wife's furniture—

"Mmm..." She mulled the offer and considered the flowers, then said airily, "No. I don't think a walk with you would be a good idea. Hush, Digger," she said to the puppy who was barking—just the way he had when the upstairs bed creaked while they made love.

The starched collar irritated Quinn's neck and he jerked it aside. Ophelia and Alfred, followed by other couples, promenaded slowly by, watching with interest. Ophelia waved. "Evening, Quinn. Evening, Taylor."

After smiling and waving at the elderly couple and hushing Digger, Taylor snapped at Quinn, "Go away. I'm getting ready for my run."

"You already did that." He showed his teeth. His mother was keeping Keely, and he was prepared to wait all night.

"Oh, all right," Taylor said, finally opening the door. Digger began sniffing at Quinn's jeans, inspecting the new starchy scent. "Why are you here? Make it fast." She buried her face in the flowers, frowning up at him. "And I did not have a 'buzz on.' *And I have never been pulled into a man's lap.* Before I leave this town in two weeks, I am going to make a stand at that pub and *leave without you embarrassing me.*"

He realized he would have to tread delicately. He decided he had said enough at this point, and he handed her a small package. Taylor looked at it as though it were a bomb. "Keely tied the bow," she noted. "Please tell her I think it's very pretty. It's obvious you're trying to apologize for your... your behavior this afternoon."

She stopped and sniffed the air between them delicately, frowning. "Quinn, why is Digger smelling your jeans? Do you smell something burning?"

"No. Open your present," he prodded, too roughly, edging Digger aside with his boot. The puppy returned to his sniffing immediately. Quinn noted the remnants of what resembled a chewed bra dangling from the back of a chair. He closed his eyes briefly against the memory of Taylor standing in the bedroom, dressed in nothing but her thigh-high stockings.

She hesitated, sniffed once, then placed the flowers aside. She picked curiously at the package, opening it. When the small, hand-carved leprechaun emerged, perched on a shamrock-shaped walnut base, Taylor's face lit up, and Quinn released the air he'd been holding in his lungs. "Oh, how beautiful."

He closed his eyes when she stroked the carving, remembering light, curious fingertips touching him intimately. Her hand wrapped around the leprechaun, drawing his leering face to her chest, and Quinn almost melted.

"You made this," she exclaimed delightedly, her dimples deepening. Then, her eyes darkened. "It won't work," Taylor said gently, holding the smiling leprechaun against her breasts as if he might leap away. The soft mounds beneath her leotard pressed upward, creamy and damp from exercise.

Quinn closed his eyes again, perspiration beading his upper lip. She peered up at him, her hand touching his arm. He noted with satisfaction that she kept the leprechaun pressed against her tightly...where Quinn wanted to be. "Quinn, are you feeling all right?" she asked warily.

No, he thought darkly as he stared down at the leprechaun leering up at him from between Taylor's breasts. He considered the taut set of his muscles. No, he wasn't all right. "I'm fine," he lied.

"Don't forget to tell Keely that her bows are beautiful," Taylor said, very formally. Quinn's instincts told him that in another minute she would be closing the old-fashioned oval glass door, and he wouldn't be inside. "The leprechaun is beautiful. I know you are very talented. Thank you," she continued, and Quinn felt himself clinging by his proverbial fingertips.

He glanced at Digger, who was dragging a long length of elastic bandage down the stairs. "Have you had supper yet?" he asked, trying a desperate shot at keeping her.

"If you're thinking of following this beautiful carving and the flowers with an invitation back to the pub for dinner, forget it," Taylor warned darkly. "When I return to the scene of your crimes, I'll go alone, and I'm walking—repeat *walking*—out by myself."

"Could I follow the flowers with a kiss?" Quinn pressed softly.

Her eyes widened, darkened. "Your kisses are *not* simple," she said finally, precisely.

Quinn lifted an eyebrow. "Could be that I'm out of practice," he admitted roughly.

She mulled that thought over, her finger stroking the carving, and Quinn's whole body began to perspire. He hoped his starch would not wilt.

Taylor studied him carefully. "Are you here to offer an apology or to try to get me to throw the race? Or are you still worried about Ferguson Lake?"

At one o'clock in the morning, Taylor slid out of bed. Earlier Quinn's head had gone back as though she'd slapped him, his eyes narrowing like a gunslinger's. But there was something else there, a shadow of pain, quickly veiled. In the next heartbeat, he had apologized stiffly and strolled off into the firefly-lit evening, taking his incredible freshly showered male scents with him, hoarding them away.

She could have shot him. Very little had kept her from dragging him back inside. Quinn had walked away when she was spoiling for a fight, needing to trim away the last edge of her mood.

She'd been working out to Chuck Berry's music, high on oxygen and the look in Quinn's eyes when he'd pulled her into his lap earlier.

At thirty-five, she'd never been pulled into a man's lap.

Quinn had an exceptionally comfortable lap. Finding him thrusting beneath her hips and his mind-boggling kiss was enough to shatter any woman. She'd been startled and passionately aroused, straddling him and edging closer to his desire. The big grins lined up from Blarney's best had destroyed any chance for recovery. Embarrassed by her actions more than by Quinn's, she'd retreated from the battlefield.

Tired of waiting for the dawn, Taylor scanned the lake and hoped for just one sighting of the baby Loch Ness.

The lake lay quiet and dark and safe, the moon hovering over the rounded Arkansas hills.

Because she wanted to feel the cool, moist air on her skin, she dressed slowly in a loose long dress, a cotton print supported by an elastic bodice and two shoulder straps. Fearing that Digger would run into the brambles and be hurt, she left him in the safety of the back porch.

Mist hovered over the millpond as she walked slowly across the tiny arched bridge. There was no reason she should apologize to him. Then why did she feel she had wounded him?

Taylor reached her hand out into the mist, capturing the cool air. A big, rough hand wrapped around her wrist, warming it, as Quinn loomed over her. She tried to speak, but then his palm was lifting, fitting her mouth to his in a long, sweet, hungry kiss.

Taylor had wanted this, the sweet brushing of his lips across hers, the gentle, safe touch. She'd fought entanglements her entire adult life, and now, if she didn't have this one moment with Quinn, she'd disintegrate. Taylor clung to him, wrapping her arms around his neck and resting against him as he picked her up and carried her into the mill.

Quinn held her tightly against him as though he feared she would run away.

She held him tighter, her lips resting on the hard pulse at his throat as he swept her up the stairs.

His bedroom was still, cool, scented with wood, the moonlight spreading across his rumpled bed. He placed her on her feet gently. "If you're going to leave me, do it now," he whispered roughly, his hands cupping her breasts, thumbs sweeping across the tender tips.

"I'm not leaving," she returned, her stomach quivering. She placed her hand on his shoulder, stroking the hard flow of muscles beneath her fingertips.

Quinn lowered his mouth to brush against hers, back and forth, lingering, pressing, teasing. Then he smoothed away the dress, kissed each bare shoulder and gathered her to him.

They stood in the moonlight, holding, smoothing, caressing. "You're a very gentle man," she whispered against his throat, her fingers trailing along the waistband of his jeans, tracing the snap.

Quinn smiled against her cheek, the rough scrape of his beard tingling on her skin. He didn't feel gentle. He trembled, holding back the stark need to take her quickly, then come back for a second leisurely helping. His instincts told him to devour her, to make her remember what they shared. But he wouldn't.

He'd made a mistake the first time, allowing her to race through lovemaking and taking him with her.

She'd been too tight, too hot. Her slight grimace of pain wouldn't happen tonight.

Quinn began to sweat as Taylor's smooth breasts gently etched an erotic pattern against his skin. Her tongue traced his lips, flicking his teeth, and Quinn gathered her closer.

Taylor tugged the snap at his jeans, but failed to open it. Then her hand traced him gently, timidly, and Quinn forgot his intentions, ripping away his snap, allowing the jeans to drop away.

When she touched him, Quinn's body lurched, heat racing through him. He promised himself he would take things slowly. Then Taylor looked down, stroking him, her slight frown of concentration scaring the hell out of him.

He wanted her to take all the time she needed, despite his desperation to be wrapped in her, to let her take away the cold. No other woman had warmed him—he knew that now as her eyes widened, her fingers gliding softly over the shape of him.

She was soft, so soft. A curl drifted along his cheek, and he shuddered, easing one knee to the bed and drawing her down with him.

Taylor rippled against him, slanting her lips over his, drawing his mouth against hers. "Ah...Quinn...if you'd rather not..." she offered hesitantly. "I know I...I'm probably not what you want—"

He tugged her hair, drawing her face up to him. "What?"

"You seem so reserved," she whispered unevenly. "As though you're pacing yourself, when I—"

"The hell I am," he exploded softly, allowing them to fall into his bed.

He spread Taylor across him, allowing her time to remember who he was and that he had not hurt her. Holding her soothed him, filled the emptiness as no other woman had. He wanted her to feel safe, to realize in her deepest being that they had already made love once and that more would follow. He lifted her slightly, trailing kisses down her throat to her smooth breasts. "Your breasts are perfect, Tay," he whispered, scoring them gently, equally, with his teeth.

She shivered, hiding her hot face in his throat. "You don't have to say that, Quinn."

He kissed the dark tips of her breasts, caressing them one at a time, kissing the slope and the rounded sides of her softness, treasuring her slowly. "Beautiful."

"Quinn—" She shivered, unable to look at him, as he stroked the delicate skin with his rough hands. "Oh, Quinn, I want you," she whispered, and the bare sound rocketed through him.

He gathered her closer, ordering himself not to hurry, to allow her time. Her stomach was smooth, gently rounded, flowing into the dark nest of curls between her thighs. She inhaled, holding him tightly, her body tense.

"That's right, Tay," he whispered, easing his hand over her, cupping her. "Hold on tight to me."

She shifted up against him, and Quinn sucked in his breath, gritting his teeth. When they made love the first time they had barely started to fit and she had taken him by surprise. Now Taylor's hips moved against him, following the gentle rocking of his hand, his fingers.

Her teeth nipped his earlobe, and he jumped.

Taylor laughed softly, the sound floating on the night. Her thighs moved like liquid silk, restlessly, against his. "You are marvelous," she whispered shakily, raising over him as she had the afternoon before.

"Tay, wait..." he cautioned roughly as she positioned herself gently upon the very tip of him.

He closed his eyes, willing himself not to move. The warm, moist, tight enclosure began contracting around him instantly. Taylor's expression was tense, as she drew the pleasure into herself. Quinn steeled himself, concentrated on making the night last him for eternity, and watched the beautiful awe spread across her face again.

She had given herself to him. To his care. "Tay?" he whispered when she lay with her head on his shoulder, her breathing unsteady.

"Tay?" Was she frightened? He kissed her damp forehead, rocking her.

She shuddered delicately, gathering him closer, holding on to him as if he were a lifeline. He eased deeper, stretching her gently until he filled her tightly. He promised himself he would lie quietly, letting her adjust to him.

They had the night, he told himself, holding her closer.

"Quinn...you're not...enjoying this, are you?" Taylor asked hesitantly. "Am I hurting you?"

"I'm dying," he returned truthfully with a grin as she stroked and kissed his chest. Reassured by his tender stroking hand, she continued exploring him. When she found his nipple, suckling it gently, he arched upward.

The storm swirled around them, heating, licking, taking them into the center. Quinn gathered her closer, fighting to hold her with him, fearing that she would leave.

He cradled her against him, unwilling to move his legs from the soft drape of hers. She settled down at his side, snuggling to him, one leg tangled between his. "You cried out," she whispered in the darkness.

Quinn nibbled her lips. "So did you."

The dark shadows enclosed them, the reflection of the water from the millpond playing on the ceiling.

"Making love with you is very beautiful," she said distinctly.

Her hand rested on his stomach, stroking the line of hair there with her fingertip. "I've never spared time or thought for this, Quinn. You may not know this, but I'm not very good at involvements...relationships. I've never wanted them. This is very...very intimate."

"Very." He closed his eyes, luxuriating in her scents, in their scents, in the soft, warm tangling of their bodies. Taylor trailed kisses to his mouth, her hair falling around him like a silky, fragrant veil.

"You're a very pliable man, Quinn," she noted, rubbing her cheek against his rough one, nuzzling him. At the moment, Quinn felt about as pliable as stone.

"Uh-huh," he murmured as she rubbed the arch of her foot up and down his calf.

His body was already straining, wanting more. "Quinn, I didn't know it would be like this, so soft and gentle."

"Uh-huh," he agreed between his teeth, his hand cupping her soft derriere. He liked the classy word when it was applied to Taylor's backside. He placed his hands over her and gripped possessively, closing his eyes.

He inhaled, realizing that his hands were trembling, filled with her, and that he'd forgotten to touch lightly. He waited, barely breathing, fearing for her and caressing her lightly. In another minute, she'd leave. But she didn't move away, just settled neatly in his palms.

"Here we are, lying together, chatting away," she continued airly, smoothing his stomach. She passed her hand lower and jerked it back when she discovered his hardened body. "You know, Quinn, I feel like running. Trims away a

ot of nervous energy. Do you feel like an early-morning
un?''

"No..." he said slowly, fitting his hands around her waist
and rubbing his thumbs across her stomach, tracing her
hipbones. "Not really."

Her eyes were tender. "You are so gentle, Quinn. I should
have known by the way you handle Keely."

She toyed with his hands, fitting them over her breasts,
studying the effect of his dark skin against her pale softness. When he caressed her gently, she closed her eyes.
"Thank you. I'm not that experienced, and all I needed was
a gentle, understanding man. I'm certain I won't have any
problems with my sexuality now," she said firmly, as though
she had just graduated at the top of the class. "To be truth-
ful, I have been afraid to try this, but now you've given me
the confidence. I don't think I'll need that therapy session
when I get back in the swing of things."

Quinn didn't want to think about her leaving. Or exploring what they had shared with another man. His hands slid
to tighten on her waist. "Tay, are you thinking you might
want to try this with someone else?"

She stroked his tense thighs, her fingers drifting over him,
exploring. "Well, you've shown me that lovemaking can be
beautiful...euphoric, even."

"...'Euphoric,' as in 'this is rather okay'?" he repeated
darkly. "So you think that you might try this gentle, euphoric lovemaking thing with another man?"

She lightly, experimentally, touched the tip of him with
her finger, and he jerked against her. "You're only my second experience, Quinn. The first was horrible. You don't
understand. I didn't think I would ever be able to...to...you
know...without therapy."

Quinn thought about her delicate contractions around
him, her startled expression—her 'you know's. At this moment, his fists knotted in the tangled sheets, he wanted her
again. She'd be too tender, he reminded himself, straining
to keep from tossing her beneath him.

"So you have horrible and euphoric. Plain old bland euphoric," he said, nettled.

Taylor cuddled against him, stroking his ribs and nuzzling the hair on his chest to find his nipples. She bit them lightly and sighed, her leg sliding up and down his. "Let's go for that run, Quinn. It should trim off any excess energy."

His fingers tightened around her wrist, jerking her to him. "So you're not afraid of me, Tay. Good old euphoric, okay Quinn, hmm?"

She looked down at him uncertainly. "Well, yes. There are times when you strike me as untamed, and there are those moody scowls. But when we…now, you've been very nice and sweet."

"Nice. Sweet." He bit off the lukewarm words. "And now you would like to go for a little run to trim off energy after we've just made love. Tell me, Tay darlin', are you hurting in any way?"

She considered the question. "No, I feel wonderful. But I seem to be a bit restless. Running always seems to straighten things out, and I can sleep better."

"Straighten things out," Quinn repeated grimly, and decided that was an apt phrase for the way he felt now.

She peered down at him, clearly puzzled. "Quinn, why are you repeating everything I say?"

He countered her question with his own. "Tay, darlin', have you ever bathed with a man?"

"Of course not." She mulled the concept over with a frown, then brightened. "No…no, I can't say I have." She smiled delightedly, her dimples shadowing in the early dawn. "Oh, Quinn, could we?"

Nine

"This isn't a date," Taylor said to Digger, who tilted his head curiously as she smoothed her new summer dress. He continued to lie and chew on his toy as she turned in front of the bedroom mirror. "Quinn is just walking with me to his parent's house for their Friday family supper. Try not to chew anything that can't be replaced while I'm gone."

She crushed the small pink rose print on her full skirt. Then, forcing her fingers to open, she smoothed the print against her thigh. She cleared her throat, angling the line of her body into the oval standing mirror. The dress's sweetheart neckline and bare shoulders led into a slender waist and a short full skirt that swirled around her legs when she walked. The dress was a whim, ordered to go with Blarney's old-fashioned country nuances.

Taylor glanced at the two leprechauns on her bedside table. She tilted her head, studying the one Keely had brought on her afternoon tricycle ride. Both fairy elves' expressions reminded her of Quinn's cocky grin as he'd lain stretched out beneath her. "I could have walked there by myself, you know, boyos," she told them. "But it seemed to be a massive point with Quinn. I didn't want to argue at the moment."

After mind-blasting, body-blasting lovemaking, Quinn had settled her limp, sated body against his and told her stories of dragons and elves that would have seduced the coldest heart . . . punctuating the fascinating bits of folklore with tender kisses.

Fairy tales would get to her every time, Taylor thought, her eyes darkening in the mirror. At one point, somewhere about her inner knees, Quinn had made an obscure, wistful comment about playing dragon and elves with her. She'd been too dreamy and tired to ask what he meant.

She smoothed the strands of hair that had been tucked high away from her face and let them cascade down her back. She didn't look like Winscott's Steel Hart, the mechanical woman.

She didn't look like a woman who'd remained stunned while Quinn walked her home at dawn. She didn't look like a woman who had slept until one o'clock in the afternoon. Or a woman who had kept a man pinned beneath her through most of the early-morning hours.

Taylor frowned, smoothing a tender, chafed spot on her throat that she had covered with cosmetics. With a flush that hadn't stopped since she awoke, slightly tender lips and a lazy, grinning, well-fed-cat feeling inside her, she looked like a woman who was waiting for her lover.

"This isn't really a date," Taylor repeated firmly. "Though I've only had a few dates, I'm certain this definitely isn't one."

She'd never slept past seven at the latest, and that had been after a fatiguing all-night business negotiating session.

Quinn had not negotiated. He had been urgent, untamed, sweet, tender, hungry, sensitive. But after the startling realization that the bath preceded Quinn's other plans, he had taken her with determination. He had seduced her,

made love to her with desperation, and then softly, long-
ingly, as if he wanted the morning to last for an eternity.

The puppy flopped down on the floor, muzzle resting on
his paws, listening to her. "If I live for another century, I
will never forget the sight of Quinn bringing me morning
coffee in bed. He was outrageous, you know. That skimpy
towel barely covered his hips. A morning schedule like that
could be addictive."

Lying beside him in the morning, his arm tucked leisurely around her waist as they shared their morning coffee
could be addictive. She frowned and tugged at the sweetheart neckline, noting that she had gained a few pounds.
She felt as if she could fend off twenty Jamisons. Quinn had
given her back something she'd needed for years. A tender
taste of romance, of hunger—

Yet something still bothered her. Quinn wrapped big, fat
secrets around him like a shroud, or a knight's armor, refusing to give her the slightest tidbit of information regard-
ing his marriage, while he knew everything about her.

She slipped into the flat shoes that matched the dress,
studying them. They didn't have one chew mark, and they
looked suited to a summer evening's walk. They suited the
dress.

She always wore business pumps or running shoes. Taylor inhaled, pushing down the panic rising within her.

What was she doing?

She was not a country girl preparing for a date with her
first beau.

She was Winscott's "Steel Hart," the mechanical businesswoman. Since her teens, she had enveloped herself in
succeeding at business, and nothing else. The obsession to
stay free of relationships had seemed to drift away amid the
magnolia and scents of Blarney.

Quinn came from another world, a world of families and
malt shops, where time rolled around when it rolled around.
Where Keely's scraped knee, and the color and size of the
bandage on it, were the concern of everyone.

Taylor stopped pacing and touched the bow Keely had tied around the lephrechaun's neck. She had little or no experience with children.

What was she doing? Taylor smoothed the skirt again and walked slowly down the stairs.

Why had she agreed to have dinner with his parents? She knew why. Quinn could charm a dead toad into agreeing to hop. "Honestly. Grown people playing dragons and elves..."

The whole scenario was too overpowering, much more frightening than a board of directors calling her on the carpet for a decision to spend money on long-term profits.

She didn't fit into this community. Or into Quinn's life. The sooner she packed Maudie's things— Taylor looked around the lovely house, saw the summer breeze tugging at the curtains, the teapots lined up and shining. Packing Maudie's things away would be difficult. She shuddered at the thought of hired movers packing away the delicate possessions.

Then there was Ferguson Lake and Baby and the shad. If anything happened to Blarney because of her... Taylor smoothed her palms against her dress. None of this was happening. She'd dropped into a dream.

Suddenly Quinn loomed outside the frosted pane of the front door, filling it, and her heart raced. He spoke quietly to Keely, a small shape leaning against his leg, and the rumbling deep tones started Taylor tingling. Beyond the lace covering the oval window, he knelt and smoothed Keely's hair and turned her around, tugging at her ruffled skirt.

Taylor's stomach ached and her entire body softened while Digger leaped against the door and yipped happily.

Quinn rang the bell, and the alarm set off tingling up and down her spine.

When she opened the door, Digger barreled out of it to frolic around Keely's legs. She giggled, and Quinn smiled. It wasn't his usual cocky, quick grin. Rather, it was a wary, soft, slightly shy smile that warmed her from head to toe.

Dressed in a light summer shirt and worn but pressed jeans, Quinn looked cool and calm, unlike the devastating moment when he— Taylor pushed away the thought of his lovemaking uneasily.

Keely grinned and held the puppy, who was squirming, angling for a way to lick her cheek. "Daddy said I look very pretty. Like a princess. You look pretty, too. We came to get you and take you to my grandma's house for our date. She said she's a-dither 'cause my daddy has never brought home his girlfriends before—"

She frowned up at her father, who had just nudged her with his knee. She held out a bouquet of flowers for Taylor. When she took them, Quinn kept a small red rose and tucked it in Taylor's hair.

His dark green eyes slowly took in her dress. "Evenin', Tay darlin'," he said very formally, despite the fires raging in his eyes.

"Evening, Quinn... Evening, Keely," she returned breathlessly as he bent to kiss her lightly.

Then Keely was taking her hand, tugging her down to replace Quinn's firm kiss with a juicy, soft one. "Evening, Tay."

"Ready?" Quinn asked, as if he'd been picking Taylor up this way all their lives. Then he drew her out the door, reaching past her to close it. He kissed her ear and nipped the lobe gently.

"Can we take Digger?" Keely asked, placing the puppy on the porch.

"I... Yes, we can," Taylor said. Quinn snapped the leash lying on the porch onto the puppy's collar and handed it to Keely.

When Taylor finally caught her breath, they were strolling down the sidewalk, their fingers laced. Keely held Digger's leash and kept a firm hold on her other hand. The puppy behaved as though trained, prancing ahead, tail arced high over his back.

"Evening," Ophelia and Alfred and the rest of the promenaders on Hummingbird Lane said, meeting them on the sidewalk.

"Evenin'," Quinn returned, nodding. He handed Keely and Taylor safely to the cobblestones, allowing the elderly couples to pass on the sidewalk.

"Taking your best girls to your folks' place for Friday-night dinner?" Alfred asked, his eyes twinkling.

"Sure am. Churning ice cream later. Cade's best cream cow is serving."

Taylor wondered if she had dropped into a previous century as Keely curtsied for the courtly elderly promenaders.

"Race still on?" Thomas Journey asked, his wife's white-gloved hand on his crooked arm.

"Sure is. Early night tonight. Have to rest up for ten o'clock in the morning," Quinn returned, caressing her palm with his hand. She stared up at him and wondered why she was dressed in a cotton print dress—something she'd never owned. She wondered why she had a puppy showing off for the promenaders and why a little girl's hand clung to hers and why she had spent the morning hours in Quinn's arms?

She was a top CEO, a negotiator. She worked twenty-hour days when necessary. Her world was computers, telephones, secretaries, and files and flights. She'd never stayed long enough in one place to have a pet. Nor had she wanted one. There were months at a time when she lived out of her carry-on luggage and her briefcase.... They called her Winscott's "Steel Hart"....

"Hot one tomorrow night, they say," Alfred noted, tugged along by Ophelia, as he was blocking the line of strolling couples. "Storm coming in. Should hit tomorrow night."

Ophelia beamed at the three of them standing on the cobblestones. Quinn held Taylor's right hand and Keely held her left. "Maudie would have been so happy," Ophelia murmured, her eyes starry. "You're just perfect for Blarney Flats, Taylor. And it's good for you. You're looking so much better than when you arrived. My, Digger is behaving well."

"Come along now, Ophelia. You have your own beau to keep happy with that cherry pie of yours," Alfred returned.

"Alfred, we've been married almost seventy years. If you keep calling yourself my beau, people will start talking," his wife cooed.

Taylor blinked when she found herself wondering if she could build a cherry pie.

The Donovan farmhouse lay just beyond Blarney Flats' outskirts, a white two-story house sheltered by tall oaks. Fields spread out behind the house, and a tire swing hung in the front yard.

"Quinn," Taylor began uncertainly as Keely skipped on ahead, to be plucked up in Cade's arms. "I don't know about this."

"What?" He had his arm around her now, drawing her close to him. She moved uneasily away, only to be drawn back.

"You know what this looks like . . . like you're bringing home your girlfriend. I am not that."

"Uh-huh. You're not."

She eyed him. "You gave up too easy."

"Uh-huh." He nuzzled her throat until she laughed, then he lifted his eyebrows twice, teasingly. "You're not my girlfriend. You're my *woman*."

A moment later, Taylor realized she was staring, her mouth open. "Quinn!"

He kissed her palm, folded her fingers over the spot and drew her hand to his heart. "Your blush becomes you, my dear," he murmured, imitating Alfred's courtly tones.

In the kitchen, Molly lifted a blackberry pie from the oven and set it aside to cool. "We're just about ready, Tay. Quinn, stop pestering the girl and get your father and Cadell," she ordered when Quinn bent to kiss the side of Taylor's throat.

Taylor jumped and fought her rising blush, and Molly beamed.

Over fried chicken, Keely's "smashed taters" and white cream gravy, new green beans seasoned with bacon and wilted garden lettuce, Taylor remained dazed. Quinn sat close and held her hand, just as though they had been coming to the Donovan's family table for years. She clung to him as if he were a lifeline as the warmth of the loving family flowed around her.

From his place of honor on the screened back porch, Digger yipped and threatened the cats roaming the yard.

Sitting near her grandfather, Keely offered to tie a bow in Taylor's hair after dinner. Cade and James argued over whose current bow was best, Cade's yellow or James's red. Molly mourned her dinner, saying it needed the juicy Arkansas tomatoes that weren't quite ripe.

They discussed the watermelons growing "in the bottoms," Ben Tully's chickens, and the best kind of sweet corn for eating and freezing.

Taylor spoke when necessary. She had cut herself away from family ties just as soon as she could, and she'd never missed them...until now. This family was very close, speaking of Cade's and Quinn's antics as boys, of Bria's first high school prom. The local football hero had made a pass at her, and the next morning the Donovan boys had called him out, embarrassing Bria, who had already defended herself. For revenge, she had enticed skunks into Cade's and Quinn's cars.

"I think I like Bria," Taylor said, laughing outright, and Quinn turned to her, studying her closely.

"Tay has dimples," he announced clinically, as though listing her selling points.

"Okay. I've got dimples. I'm also very fast," she returned smugly. "I'll be first across the finish line tomorrow. You just keep eating second helpings of those nice heavy potatoes, boyo."

Cade and James laughed outright. Then Quinn murmured, "Perhaps I will waylay you along the way, Tay darlin'."

"If I win," she replied, upping the challenges running between them, "you will have to pay. There's cleaning the basement and weeding the garden."

"If I win," he challenged, taking her hand, "you'll be my partner at the picnic after the race. That is, after the toss I'm giving you in the lake. Then I think you should serve my every whim at the picnic. Fetch and carry, that sort of thing."

"When *I* win," Taylor began determinedly, "you will find a way to introduce ladies to the men-only hour."

Quinn snorted. "Not likely. The men-only hour is a God-given, male tradition."

"When I win," Keely said, squirming between them and looping an arm around Taylor's and Quinn's necks, "I'm getting my lephrechaun to get me a mommy like the other kids at vacation Bible school."

There was a stiff moment of silence, then Quinn's eyes darkened as he gathered her up in his lap and rocked her.

After dinner, the "busboys," Quinn and Cade, cleared the table, directed by Molly.

"Come on out to the backyard, Tay," James invited, carrying out a steel cylinder filled with "ice-cream makin's." "Help me start the ice cream."

He locked the cylinder into a wooden bucket and poured a mixture of ice and salt around it. "Let's sit a spell," he said, easing into a wooden lawn chair. "The boys will be out in a minute to churn."

He leaned back in the lawn chair, while she sat in another, feeling very out of place, as she had all evening. "So, you're wondering about Quinn. And I'll wager he hasn't told you a drop," James said. "A man, almost forty, with one small, sweet child to raise by himself."

His expression darkened in the shadows. "He'll tell you when it's time, and that time is coming close I'd say. You're a strong, good woman, Tay. You do what you think is right.

Maudie would have liked you. You're like her, a woman who makes choices and sticks by them."

Taylor followed a blinking firefly across the lawn. "He's a talented man."

"Quinn? Yes." James's eyes followed Keely, who was tying a bow on his best beagle's tail. "He set out of here like a steam engine, ready to make his mark. We heard from him regularly, and he came home when he could. Then he met his ex-wife, and Quinn changed. We saw it happening. The letters stopped. We could tell by his once-in-a-while phone calls that something was wrong. Then, a few years later, he turned up with Keely—she was six months then—and one bag of her necessaries. He'd hitched from God only knows where. There he stood under the light of the front porch— thin, looking half-dead, with a pretty little baby girl in his arms. Never asked, and he never said what happened. But whatever it was, it nearly tore the soul out of him. That was over three years ago. In the last week he's been fiddling with architect's drawings again, and I'd say you are the reason. Quinn doesn't let people in easily now, but you're there—in him. You've been good for him."

"I leave in just over a week," Taylor said.

"Then you do," James said firmly, watching Digger run after a cat until she stopped. The puppy plopped his bottom on the grass as the cat leisurely licked its paws. "We'll miss you. If the heart is willing, you'll come back. If not, you gave my boy something pretty special to last him."

Then Quinn was lifting her, settling himself in the chair and holding her on his lap. "You churn, Cade. I'm entertaining."

"You know, Donovan, I am not a sack of potatoes," she stated archly when she could speak, tugging down her skirt. "There are neat little chops and kicks and things that I can do to stop this constant manhandling."

"Womanhandling," Quinn corrected with a leer.

Unused to being taken lightly, she stared at him. "Donovan...you need help. The caveman era is over."

He sighed mournfully, laying his head on her shoulder. "Don't I know it! Women keep forgetting they are supposed to fetch and carry— Whoof!" The jab of her elbow sank into his stomach.

He held her tightly, tickling her and nuzzling her neck, using growling hungry-bear noises. When Taylor finally was allowed to stop giggling and catch her breath, Quinn snuggled her closer against him. "There. Stay put," he ordered in a satisfied tone, kissing the side of her neck where he had just nuzzled.

Taylor sat very still. She had never giggled in her life. The family accepted Quinn's teasing, but she wasn't certain how to respond. She'd have to work on teasing, Taylor decided. Quinn was too confident.

"You're trying to make points with Tay, so she'll feel sorry for your poor out-of-shape—" Cade grinned and crouched to turn the handle of the churn.

"Derriere?" Quinn supplied innocently as he smoothed hers stealthily beneath the skirt.

Keely climbed onto his other knee and began tying a length of pink ribbon in Taylor's hair. "Daddy has me sit on his back while he does push-ups. We count how many he can do before he lays down to rest. He gets hot and breathes hard. Then he has a button thing that shows how fast he can run. I push when he runs and when he stops I push another button. It's fun. Sometimes he carries me when he runs. He says he's working on pri…priorities. He says he is 'one fast son of a gun,' and just as good as he used to be."

"Aha! Donovan, you *are* out of shape," Taylor said, gloating.

"Temporarily, Tay darlin'," he said with a wicked look that reminded her of the early-morning hours, and Taylor began to wonder if her blushes would become permanent.

Then Keely started to scamper off to play with Digger and James's new puppies, but Quinn drew her closer, nestling his cheek against hers. He wasn't playing now, but holding her close and rocking her as if she were very precious to him.

Taylor closed her eyes, inhaling the dreamy night air. No matter what secrets he held, tonight was perfect, a gift she would remember forever. Quinn had given her this safety, the long, easy evening and his family's warmth to wrap around her. "Sometimes I like you," she murmured honestly, placing her hands over his.

He kissed her lightly, softly, and when she opened her eyes, Cade grinned and Molly beamed, wiping a tear from her eye with the corner of her apron. James nodded. "You'll do just fine, Tay," he said roughly, clearing his throat.

When the evening was over, Keely insisted on walking Taylor home from their date. At the front porch, Quinn held his sleeping daughter against him and bent to give Taylor a long, sweet, hungry kiss. "Let's take it a day at a time, Tay," he said huskily against her ear.

"This is too much, Quinn," she returned in a whisper, dazed by the entire evening. She wasn't Midwest America. She understood schedules and negotiations and business, not things like waiting for the freshly churned ice cream to "ripen." They came from different worlds, and right now she wanted the safety of hers. "You're acting like...like we're committed. I really don't know you, and you don't know me. All this is much too fast. I can't do this—ice-cream suppers, picnics... What do I wear to a picnic? I mean—what's the protocol?" she asked, panicked, as he drew her close against him and rocked his daughter and her.

She leaned against him, slightly uncomfortable with his cherishing, but needing it desperately. "Oh, Quinn, when I look at your family—how warm and close they are—I know that I've never really had one. I left home when I was seventeen, put myself through college and never missed having a family—until now."

She reached to smooth Keely's cheek. "Quinn, I wanted my baby. You were right to bring Keely here, where there is so much love. Children need every ounce possible."

"What about you, Tay?" Quinn asked against her temple, still holding her close against him, rocking her and Keely. "There is enough love here for you."

She turned her face to his throat. "I don't think I'm good at loving."

"It's just one day, Tay. Live it," he said simply as Keely sighed. "Stay with me tomorrow night."

Watching him carry Keely on the path to the millhouse, Taylor remembered Maudie's note. *Make time for love...*

At eleven o'clock, Taylor walked to the lake, picking over the stones under her bare feet as she was picking over her thoughts. She didn't belong in Blarney Flats. She'd geared her life to business associates and a few close friends, not family. She knew how to organize a business conference, not how to prepare a dinner or make strawberry jam and lime pickles. She wasn't a woman to be picked up for a date, to wear a cotton summer dress with a flounced skirt or to go skinny-dipping in the lake.

She watched the lake, scanning for a look at the Loch Ness baby. "Sleep tight, Baby," she whispered, wishing nothing could harm him or any of these dear people.

Quinn stopped stretching his legs and watched Taylor jog leisurely toward him through the shadows of the city park's great oaks. She smiled and waved, her ponytail bobbing, to the people who called out to her. She wore her sunglasses, round dark mirrors perched on her nose, her yellow running outfit and a cocky grin. "Morning, Quinn. Great day for a run, eh?"

"Uh-huh. And when I win, I'm going to find out what you're wearing beneath your shirt."

"What?"

He bent to kiss her, savoring the sweet, stunned parting of her lips. "Your beautiful breasts are far too flat, my love," he whispered against her ear. "When I win, I'm peeling whatever you're wearing away with my teeth and nibbling on you from head to toe. I might even suck a toe or two. You're spending the night with me."

"Quinn!" Then, because she looked so shocked, the cocky grin slipping, he whipped off his T-shirt and tossed it aside. The hungry, darkened expression sweeping over Taylor's face, the set of her body, as though she'd like to pounce on him, sent Quinn's ego soaring.

For years, he hadn't cared if another woman looked, or touched, or kissed, but Taylor's delight made him want to run off with her.

She tilted her head up at him. "Just how fast are you?"

Quinn thought of running up and down stairs at night while Keely slept, of running around the back pasture until he sprawled breathless in the haystack, and of soaking his aching muscles in steamy water. With luck and a little cheating, he might just win. "Very fast," he answered. "Fast as the wind that blows in your bedroom window."

"A mere breeze. A very slow breeze. I'm upping the bet," she said, not moving away as he tugged her headband away, freed her ponytail and began braiding her hair into pigtails. Her hands rested on his wrists, and she stepped nearer. "If I win, I want two things. One, you keep Maudie's house waiting for me. I can't pack her things away. This has been the most beautiful time in my life, and I want to leave—just this once—with the house as it is. When I can, I'll come back and pack her things myself."

Quinn's heart lurched with fear. This woman had dragged him from the shadows, and now she was making plans to leave. He ran his thumb over the silky hair he had just braided. He didn't have the right to ask her to stay, this fiercely independent woman who taunted him and made him laugh, who made him remember the love and passions of his dreams long ago. But he'd be waiting when she came back. "I will. There's no reason to wager, Tay. Maudie's home will be here for you when you come back."

"Now for the second thing," she continued slowly. "I want you to get back to your dreams, to draw plans, beautiful plans for buildings...then see that they are built. I'll help you, Quinn. You're a talented man."

He studied his hands, felt the tools and rulers moving in them, the paper beneath, stretched out, waiting for his work. "It's not that easy."

"You can, Donovan. I know you can," Taylor whispered. "You've given me so much, given me a piece of my life back, and more. You can...."

Their eyes locked with promises for the night to come. But it would be hours until Quinn could hold her the way he wanted. She looked like a girl, he thought, tucking a daisy in her braid while the crowd called to them. "We could slip away, Tay darlin'," he offered, running his finger across her lips.

Her eyebrows shot up, and she stepped back, jogging toward the starting line. "You'll have to catch me first. I'll bet you're slow as molasses," she tossed back at him over her shoulder, her dimples deepening.

"We'll see, Tay darlin'." Quinn jogged to the starting line, stopped, lifted his hands for the crowd to quiet. "Let it be known that this woman will eat my dust. When I win, she is to wait on me for the rest of the day." The Donovans cheered, the Flynns booed. The rest of the townspeople did both.

Taylor grinned. "Donovan, you're full of blarney, and you're slow. For that matter, I've never waited on a man in my life."

"Maybe it's time you started, Tay darlin'."

When the starting shot sounded, Quinn glanced at her. She wasn't playing now. She was ready to win, to succeed at her challenges. They ran side by side the first mile and a half, and Quinn gave himself to matching the stride of her long legs, of thinking of an eternity spent at her side. She breathed methodically, inhaling, blowing out. "Tay, your damned shirt is driving me crazy," he muttered at her side.

"You're sweating already, Donovan. You won't make it," she said, then glanced down at his chest. "You're not in too bad of shape. Nice pecs."

Because she reacted so wonderfully, so stunned and hungry, Quinn made them dance.

Ten

_____

"**Y**ou cheated. The only reason I'm talking to you is because Keely is so proud of you," Taylor stated as she fed Quinn a sliver of chicken with her fingertips. The moon trailed over the water to the small dock behind Maudie's, and Digger lay on his favorite tattered blanket on the lawn, watching them.

Taylor sat cross-legged beside Quinn, dressed in a gauzy print two-piece dress with an elastic neckline that drooped to reveal one bare shoulder. He lay on his side, concentrating on that gleaming curve. He noted the lack of a lingerie strap and watched the folds over her chest lift as she breathed. His fingers circled her ankle; his thumb stroked her arch lazily. The dress mocked his control, clinging to her and supported by a neckline that could be easily tugged away.

He'd walked off the city dock with her in his arms after the race, and then she'd changed into the romantic two-piece dress that tortured him. Throughout the picnic, the afternoon games and the leisurely summer evening at the park, he'd thought of little else but tearing away that dress.

He kissed her fingers and wished time would stop. "My daughter has good sense. You lost."

She plopped another chicken sliver in his mouth and dusted off her fingers. "I wonder why. Of course, you took a shortcut and ran right through that barn and the cow pasture. I hope you stepped in something very fresh."

"The rules didn't specify that portion of the route, Tay darlin'. Come here."

"Working hours are over for your slave." She tossed her head, and Quinn caught one braid to gently draw her down for a long, sweet kiss. "Donovan, you are dangerous," she whispered, allowing herself to be drawn into his arms.

"Mmm...and hungry," he said between kisses. She tasted better each time. He settled a hand over her stomach, caressing it and wishing for a child with her. "You eat like a workingman, Tay. Three helpings of Margaret's potato salad, and how many helpings of blackberry cobbler?"

She sniffed delicately. "I'm storing up. I'd lost a bit of weight before I arrived."

He traced the warm swell of her bottom, his hand curving at her waist and claiming her breast. There were things he wanted to "store up," too, like memories of Taylor lying in his arms. "You've put on a few pounds. You'll squash me if you decide to have your way with me." He rolled to tug up the blouse, kiss her stomach and lick her navel before leaning over her.

"You're not that fragile.... I saw you lift that dresser by yourself. You made me wait and fetch and carry for you all day. I should shove you in the lake. But Baby isn't up to your antics, and it's my duty to protect him." She answered his kisses, deepening them as he drew away the gauzy material.

She held him close over her, stroking his back and smoothing his hair. Her bare foot slid up and down his calf. Quinn luxuriated in the smooth push of her breasts against him, the tender moment he'd waited for throughout the day.

Taylor instinctively knew how to cuddle, despite the reserve clinging to her. He smiled against her throat. Nothing could have kept him from showing off—lifting the refinished bureau to the back of Fred Jones's truck—when Taylor was watching, her expression fascinated. He admitted to flexing a muscle or two, showing off like a boy for his best girl.

Sir Elmo bellowed, and Taylor playfully bit Quinn's lip. "Ghosts. You should be ashamed," she whispered, reminding them of what he'd told her the night she arrived.

"Oh, I am, Tay," he agreed solemnly.

"Beast. You are outrageous. Imagine walking off the city's dock into the lake with me, then telling me that Baby liked to munch on offerings bigger than the carp."

"I'm despicable." Quinn kissed her jawline, giving her a necklace of kisses as he remembered Taylor clinging to him. She had dunked him and swum toward Maudie's dock. Quinn had matched her strokes as the crowd cheered and placed bets from the town's dock. Then he'd dived down, tugged her ankle and pulled her beneath the lake's surface.

Taylor's hands found the opened snap of his jeans, then swept them away. "I'm going to pay you back for that underwater kiss," she said firmly, inspecting his body as if looking for a place to start her revenge. She began by smoothing his stomach, and Quinn sucked in his breath as her fingers wandered lower.

"You're shocking Baby," Quinn murmured, running his hands down her, then leaning over her again.

He wanted to ask her to stay, to share his life. Taylor tugged him down over her, and Quinn held very still, waiting for her to move away. His heart raced as she smoothed his shoulders, skimming delicately along his chest. She looked up at him as he ran his fingers through her braids, loosening them. "This is good," he said, meaning it.

"Yes." Taylor's eyes swept over him, her kisses brushing his cheeks, his eyes. Her fingers wove through his hair, easing him closer.

He held his breath, sensing that she was making a decision, and prayed that it wasn't to leave him now. Or before the week was finished. "Are you frightened, Tay?" he asked unevenly, searching her expression for fear as she moved restlessly beneath him.

"Not of you." Then she was holding him close and kissing his throat. "Quinn, make it right, love me this way...." Caressing her gently from shoulder to hip and back again, Quinn waited for her to adjust to his weight. Her hands moved lightly over him, exploring, tormenting....

Then Taylor moved beneath him, opening her warmth to him, and there was no waiting.

Early Monday afternoon, Taylor jerked open the door to the mill and stepped inside. "Put on a shirt, Donovan," she ordered, impatiently slapping a file against her bare legs.

Quinn turned from his sketches toward her, leaning against the table. He ignored her order, sensing whatever had brought her here wasn't the playful mood of Saturday night, or Sunday's special picnic with Keely...or Sunday night's skinny-dipping while Cade baby-sat until dawn. Fear lodged like a cold stone in his heart and slammed into his stomach.

Sweat dampened her shirt and running shorts. Taylor's dark mood matched the storm that had been hovering over the weekend and now rolled full-force, with heavy thunder and lightning. "You're in a snit, Tay. And you've been running at noon, and in the face of a bad storm front. Why?"

"*Why?*" she repeated, her voice trembling with anger. Thunder rolled, and against the dark gray rolling clouds, lightning forked down to the lake. She threw out a hand, pacing the length of the room. "Why? Because you're standing there, dressed in nothing but shorts. You need a wardrobe, Quinn. Maybe cutoff jeans without holes in the wrong places."

She tossed the file to the table. "This arrived in the mail. So far this morning, I've squashed Jamison's dummy buyer and found another set of surveyor stakes on Maudie's property. Some bozo with a heavy-breathing problem called me four times...."

Quinn straightened away from the counter. Men like Jamison had nasty little tactics, and Quinn hadn't installed the locks on Taylor's doors. In Blarney Flats there was little need for locks and deadbolts. Until now. "What did he say?"

"The usual things. He's probably the guy who sprayed plant killer on Maudie's roses and geraniums. They were dying, and I found the bottle nearby."

"I said, what did he say?" Quinn demanded, taking her arm. He'd seen vultures hover and hurt. A frozen blade of fear sliced through him. He was frightened now, fearing for Taylor.

She shook him off. "I've taken care of creeps like that before, Donovan." She nodded toward the file and folded her arms across her chest. "Open it."

He opened the file, scanned the clippings and the professional investigator's report. He'd seen it all before: bold newspaper print declared him unfit for his dreams, a failure. They'd followed him in his nightmares for years. Now she had seen them before he could tell her about the darkness that wrapped around his life. Quinn's stomach locked in an icy knot. He'd been living in rainbows and sunlight, and now all that was gone. He'd expected Jamison to check out his credentials. Now they lay in the file, as faded and dead as his dreams. "Okay. So what?"

Taylor threw Keely's rag doll at him. "So what? I love you, Donovan. I ordered that investigation. Force of habit. That same force of habit caused me to open the file automatically, scanning it."

He crushed the doll he'd just caught. She loved him. His heart soared, then plummeted with the next thought. "You investigated me?"

"It's what I do. I'm thorough. I like all the ends tied up neatly. When I arrived, there were just too many unanswered questions about you. Maudie had written a little

bout you, and after I met you, I suspected you might
e..."

Her eyes were wary now, glancing at him once as she
aced across the board flooring. She slapped the heavy
ranite millstone. "Okay...I'm not afraid to admit my
nistakes. At the time, I thought you might be after
Maudie's property. If you'll remember, I told you as much
t the beginning of our..."

Taylor turned, her face stark and white, a curl sticking to
er damp skin, her body taut. "Donovan, you should have
old me. A portion of a building collapsed. You were the
rchitect, and the innovative design didn't work. You took
 chance on what you believed would succeed. There is no
uilt in that. You don't have to bury your talent."

"So now you know," he said, very quietly, feeling his
reams slide away like an ocean tide sucking sand beneath
is feet. He had intended to tell her. "I built a dream, and
t died."

"There's more to it than this—" She hit the file with her
alm.

He didn't want her in his nightmare. He was shaken that
he had stepped into it before he was ready, and furious with
imself for not telling her.

"What do you know about it? About taking care of a
aby and fearing for her? Of fearing what her mother might
lo to her if you couldn't take her to safety? About leaving
er with a baby-sitter for days while I cleaned up a damned
usiness mess, then finding her unattended when I popped
n?" Quinn stated roughly as another roll of thunder
ounded very close and lightning forked across the angry
louds. Fighting the need to jerk Taylor into his arms, he
rushed a pencil in his hand, then tossed it aside.

She stood rigid with icy anger and pain.

"It's true, I've never had to worry about anyone but my-
elf. But I am capable of understanding the fears. I under-
tand we were operating on a temporary time schedule, but
..." She stopped, took a deep breath and continued. "If
ou'd cared enough, you would have told me a little about

what was so important to you—what made you what yo
were...what you are...why you're not doing what you ar
trained for. Or at least the main points," she whispere
rawly.

The edge of pain turned and slashed at him again
"Sketched them out, you mean? Neat little dissections o
why Donovan failed?"

"This material shows how talented you are, how hard yo
must have worked to achieve this level of success."

"Success?" Quinn shot back flatly. "Is that what i
was?"

He cared, all right, he decided, rummaging through hi
raw emotions. They suited the wild, growing storm closin
in on the area. He wanted this woman to have the best par
of him, his pride and confidence in building his dreams, an
they were gone.

He'd hoped for time, hoped that Taylor would under
stand and would come back to him when she could. No
her expression, frustrated, angry and confused, left him lit
tle room for hope. It would be better if they parted now
They'd shared a few days of rainbows and sunlight an
dreams, and now they were gone. "So you trusted me. I
that why you had me investigated? I'm raising my daughte
and giving her the best I can," he said, turning away fron
the tears welling in her eyes. "Take your investigations an
your crusading somewhere else."

Aching bitterly, afraid to turn, to see Taylor's stark pai
Quinn crushed the sketches he'd been working on—a drean
house overlooking Ferguson Lake. She'd said she loved him
this woman who'd given him so much. But she didn't fit i
his world. Nor did he fit into hers. "Don't forget to sa
goodbye to Keely when you leave."

A stuffed toy duck hit him in the back before Taylo
walked out. Just before she slammed the door, she state
precisely, "I have never lowered myself to throwing any
thing at anyone. You are the exception to every personal rul
I have ever made, Quinn Donovan."

* * *

Quinn rocked Keely until she slept deeply, then stood at the door of the millhouse, looking up at Taylor's house.

Every light was on at eleven o'clock at night, and he ached to hold her. He closed his eyes, and Taylor's pale, stark expression slid into his mind, the pain echoing, echoing....

He'd dared to dream of her staying, sharing Keely and another baby or two. Quinn inhaled, his heart chilling. He held Keely closer, rocking her in the night.

Keely had been too quiet when she returned from her visit with Taylor in the late afternoon. The storms had just passed, and Taylor had called Keely to have tea with her. The hour was the longest Quinn had spent in years, dreading how his daughter would react to the loss of her precious "Tay."

He didn't know who looked forward more to Taylor's promised trips back to Blarney, Keely or himself. Keely held the telephone number Taylor had given her to call whenever she wanted, especially at Queenie's teatime. During the long-distance tea party, Taylor promised to drink tea from a special gold-rimmed china cup at the same time Keely served her dolls. Digger would be staying at Ophelia's for a time, and Keely could visit him anytime she wanted. Keely had held the crumpled scrap of paper tightly as Quinn rocked her to sleep.

Maudie's basement light clicked off, and the porch light turned on. Taylor wandered out into the shadows, outlined by the light.

The heavy breather who had called Taylor could enter the house at any time. Someone had been close enough to kill Maudie's beloved roses and geraniums. Quinn wanted Taylor and his daughter in the same house, where he could protect them.

Quinn swallowed the bitter taste in his mouth. Taylor was right. He should have told her.

But the magic ran too fast and deep between them, and he'd wanted her desperately. He'd broken a few of his own

rules, like dreaming of love and happily-ever-afters. Th
damning file had shattered his dreams too soon, peeled awa
his defenses, and before he was able to control his emo
tions, he'd lashed out at her.

He inhaled slowly as Taylor stretched out her arms to th
lake. She would be saying goodbye to Baby. He smile
tightly, remembering how she had said, "my baby Locl
Ness."

A van with no lights on slid quietly toward Humming
bird hill. Taking care not to wake Keely, Quinn dialed Cade
"I need you here to take care of Keely. Come quickly an
quietly."

The van sat in the shadows, and Taylor returned slowly t
the house. Quinn counted the seconds as he waited, an
pushed away the fear lurching at him. Within ten minute
Cade jerked open the millhouse door. He had been run
ning, he breathed heavily, clad only in his shorts and boots
"No lights," Quinn said, moving swiftly past his brother
"Keely is in bed. Stay with her."

"Sure. It's that van, isn't it? Do you want me to ca
Moriarity? Or do you want me to come along?"

"Give me a minute, then call Moriarity. You stay here
They've just knocked out the street lamp." Quinn nodde
toward the van in the shadows, and the man climbing th
telephone pole. From there he would probably attach a de
vice to dial Taylor. "I want to make an impression."

The last week of August, Taylor placed the china cup i
its saucer and disconnected her end of the line. She ran he
finger around the rim of the cup. After two months awa
from her, Keely seemed to be managing the shift in he
world well. Too well.

Quinn's daughter usually called from her grandmother'
house. Today, her grandpa and her uncle Cade were work
ing on Maudie's roses and geraniums, and they would hav
to be watered carefully, because it was August and very ho
Keely had explained proudly. She would be watering them
and it was a big responsibility for a little girl.

Taylor studied the two leering leprechauns on her desk and the framed picture of Digger that Ophelia had sent. Beyond her tinted windows, Chicago baked in the afternoon sun.

When she opened the door at four o'clock in the morning on the day she'd left Blarney Flats, Quinn had been sprawled on the old rocker on Maudie's front porch. The mists swirled around the porch, waiting for dawn, enclosing her one last time with the man she had come to love. He had erased her fears, touching her gently and giving her a portion of his beautiful life, his family.

She hadn't wanted to look at him that morning, but nothing could have kept her from watching him sleep. Haggard, stubble darkening his jaw, Quinn had looked as though he'd been fighting. Taylor frowned, remembering the dark bruise running along Quinn's cheekbone and the way he'd cupped one hand with the other as though it were bruised.

Pride had kept her from touching him, easing away the wave of hair crossing his forehead. Then Digger had yelped frantically from Ophelia's backyard, and Taylor had squared her shoulders and walked to the rented car.

Taylor's fingertip tapped her reference book on the care and feeding of hummingbirds. At the time, she'd suspected he'd decided to play the royal Donovan, picking out unsuspecting Flynns and assaulting them. Her investigation of Jamison's activities had led to Hummingbird Lane and the unwanted telephone calls. The evening before she left Blarney, a brawl involving three thugs and one Quinn Donovan had occurred beneath a street lamp that had been disconnected. Her call to Moriarity confirmed that there had been a "scrap" and that Quinn had "laid out" three men who had been shuffled away to the county seat for trial. A fancy attorney had gotten them off with a high fine.

Taylor flipped to the picture of a hummingbird that looked like her visitor at Maudie's. She traced the tiny, gleaming body in the photograph. Quinn might want to forget her.

"Too bad," she told the leprechauns. "I'm not done with Mr. Donovan just yet." Taylor tightened her lips and smoothed her new red suit. Taking down Jamison and his threats had been a piece of cake compared to what she had planned for Quinn.

She loved him. He was responsible for introducing her to gentleness and to passion. She needed him to fill the emptiness that she hadn't known existed—until Quinn.

She studied Chicago, heat rippling up from the streets. Catching up on Winscott's business hadn't left her much time to think and she wanted it that way.... Until the last week, when her office had forwarded a call from Keely to her in New York. Keely had been excited, her lengthy story about catching a leprechaun continuing while Taylor sipped her tea. The china cup and saucer and tea bags had their own special carry-on case. When Keely called, Taylor had stopped working and kept her long-distance-tea-party promise.

Keely had stopped asking wistfully, "Tay, when are you coming back?" No doubt Taylor had been forgotten when Keely's new cat had kittens in Queenie's doll carriage.. and when Quinn taught Digger to shake hands with paws.

Taylor opened Maudie's note, which she kept in a small portfolio beside her. *Make time for love...*

She'd told Quinn she loved him, and he'd tossed it aside. According to Moriarity, Quinn had endangered himself for her, fighting professional toughs. He'd beguiled her with his sweet, hungry kisses, and tantalized her with his big, gentle hands. Despite the little time they'd shared, Quinn Donovan had told her in every way but one that he loved her. He couldn't kiss her and cuddle her and make her know what love was then hoard himself away. They weren't done, Quinn Donovan and herself, not by a long shot, especially since she had placed a few calls while in New York. She'd had her breathing space, but when she was finished with Donovan, he wouldn't be able to pull himself into a hole that easily.

Then there was Keely. Quinn's daughter seemed to be coping magnificently, assured that the leprechaun had done his work. Keely thought that she had her mommy hog-tied and was reeling her in. "Donovan certainly switches his affections fast enough," Taylor muttered, wondering if "Lilian-honey" had finally acquired Quinn. She thought of Quinn's nipples dancing for another woman... of him dancing and lying beneath some other woman.

Or worse. Some other woman lying beneath him and enjoying that glorious nuzzling and cuddling and other things...

Taylor scowled at the leprechauns and Digger's picture; she traced one ear, which had flopped up on top of his head. According to Quinn, he hadn't touched another woman since Keely's conception. Now, here he was on the loose, probably with "Lilian-honey" picking up what Taylor had sampled.

"I'm not one for leaving loose ends." Taylor thought of Quinn's tight rear end and crunched a note in her fist, tossed it aside and punched the buttons for her assistant's intercom. Taylor mentally listed the other things she wanted to finish, like learning how to sugar starch lace doilies from Molly, and baking cakes with the scented geranium leaves from Maudie's stash of recipes, and teaching Digger how to shake hands. "Melissa, I'm taking another trip... and you should start thinking about how to deal with Mark Johnson. He is arrogant and top-notch. He just may be Winscott's next CEO."

Returning to the scene of the crime wasn't easy, Taylor decided, pulling her rental car to a stop in front of Maudie's house at sunset the next day. It was just two months since she'd left Blarney.

September lurked in the hot, still evening air, a storm brewing on the horizon. She'd ripped away two weeks from her schedule and would pay heavily for them. An afternoon of sharing her job's basics with Mark Johnson had left him stunned. Good—he needed his ego shredded a bit.

Mark's jaw had dropped when she'd tossed him a fat take-over file, kissed him on his cheek and had walked out the door.

Taylor walked around Maudie's house, inhaling the air, the scents and the emotions that drew her back to Blarney. She tugged off her shoes and stockings, snaring the lush cool grass between her toes and locking them to the earth. This was her home. Up and down Hummingbird Lane, lights began to click on for the evening. The gristmill loomed in the evening shadows. Despite the brooding clouds, Blarney Flats was quiet, cool, soothing—perfect.

Autumn would paint its vivid reds and oranges across the rounded hills, and Taylor intended to experience the changing of the seasons. She wanted to live her life from a home, not a suitcase.

She pulled away the red tropical-print band keeping her hair away from her face and walked toward the lake. "Baby, I'm home. . . ." she called softly.

Feasting on summer insects, a big fish shot out of the water, a silver arc in the shadows, before splashing back into the lake. Ripples spread out from his entry, widening, circling the smooth, glassy water. Crickets chirped, and Sir Elmo bellowed.

"I'm home, Baby," Taylor repeated, walking out to the dock to watch night close over Ferguson Lake and Blarney. She sat cross-legged, inhaling the night and the cool, sweet scents. In the morning, she would collect Digger from Ophelia. When it was time, she would tend to Quinn.

She didn't have long to wait. Quinn moved out of the shadows, standing over her, his long, jean-clad legs spread as if ready for a fight. "What are you doing here?" he demanded, looking just as untamed and magnificent as when she first met him.

Taylor took her time answering and avoided looking at his bare chest. She wasn't ready at the moment to deal with Quinn or his dancing nipples. "I am having a nice quiet conversation with my monster. Sorry, there's not room for three."

"You can't just come back when you want, Tay darlin'. I have plans," Quinn said in that low, raspy tone that reminded her of a wolf ready to pounce. No doubt "Lilianhoney" was included in his plans.

"You are upsetting the baby," she said very stiffly, and began to rise. "Please remove yourself from the premises. Tell Keely I will call her tomorrow."

"Just like that?" Quinn said in a tone resembling a growl. He loomed over her as she stood, his hands on his hips.

Taylor dusted her hands and tried to dismiss the day's beard covering Quinn's jaw. She wanted to cradle it in her hands and draw him down for a sweet kiss. But she wouldn't. Not yet. "Just like that."

"Tay. I said I have plans," he stated warningly. He moved toward her, his expression grim. Taylor found herself stepping back, losing her balance and teetering at the edge of the dock. She reached out—

Quinn caught her wrists; Taylor fought his hold, and he lost his balance. Quinn's curse hit the still summer air before they both fell into the lake.

Taylor came up sputtering, pushing her hair away from her face. Quinn burst through the water's surface an instant later, swishing water from his head. The drops hit her in the face, and she slashed them away. They treaded water, glaring at each other. The gentle waves lapped against them. "Get out of my lake," Taylor ordered when she could speak. "*You are frightening my monster.*"

"If you wouldn't fall into things, I wouldn't have to fish you out," he returned darkly, reminding her of the blackberry-bramble incident.

"You are in the water, too, Mr. Donovan."

After a long, hard stare, Quinn reached for the dock and jerked himself to his feet. When Taylor placed her hands on the boards, he cursed, bent and placed his hands under her arms and lifted her out. Taylor shimmered with anger, barely leashing her need to push Quinn back into the lake. He had managed to tear away the carefully structured meeting she had planned with him—one that she could control, wading through the issues between them. "Get off my dock," she managed tightly.

Quinn inhaled, cursed darkly and ran his hand across his face to flip water into the lake. Then he nodded curtly and walked into the shadows. Taylor followed the sound of his squishing boots toward the millhouse and frowned. "Donovan, you give up too easily."

Eleven

"She's back?" Cade asked when Quinn walked into the millhouse.

Quinn nodded and glanced at his brother, who was leaning back on the legs of his chair and watching the lake through the open door. Dressed in boxer shorts, worn boots and a wide grin, Cade had answered his brother's call to baby-sit Keely.

"It figures. She's not the kind of woman who will wait for a man to come after her. And you've been taking your time, boyo. Two months is plenty of time for a woman to change her mind," Cade said as Quinn jerked off his wet boots and dumped the water to the floor. He tore away his wet jeans, ran a towel over his head and chest and took the stairs two at a time to retrieve dry undershorts.

"Stop grinning," Quinn ordered darkly when he returned and sat on a chair. He tipped it back and took the iced tea Cade held out to him.

"Hope your swim cooled you off, boyo. Want to talk?" Cade pressed, his grin widening. "Need advice on handling women?"

"No." Quinn didn't want to sit drinking iced tea with his brother. He wanted to make love with Taylor. He wanted to hold her in his arms and let her know that she was safe. He wanted her to know that he needed her and she belonged in Blarney when she wanted to come home. He wanted to give her the chest he'd made, the kind the Donovan men gave their brides. Of sturdy Arkansas oak and walnut, it would hold up to shipping when she moved around the country.

He wanted to tell her of his excitement, his plans, his dreams.

"A woman like that sets her own terms," Cade prodded.

"Don't you want to go home now?" Quinn returned easily as his brother chuckled.

"What? And get called over here again in the middle of the night? I think I'll just wait awhile and see if everything settles down." Cade stopped, listened, then lifted his glass to toast the sound of approaching footsteps on the arched bridge. The footsteps hit the boards, quickly crossing the bridge, and clicked firmly across the stones, nearing the millhouse.

Taylor stood in the doorway. The moon outlined the shape of her wet head and body for a moment while she found Quinn in the shadows. She dripped a path across the rough boards, walking toward him.

She stopped, stared grimly at him and held out her hand, palm up.

Quinn slapped the new lock's keys to Maudie's house into her hand.

Taylor closed her fingers over the key ring, making a tight fist as though she wanted to hit him. She frowned at him for a full minute, then straightened her shoulders and turned, walking toward the doorway. "Evening, Cade," she said firmly. "Please tell Keely that I'm home and I am expecting her first thing in the morning."

When her footsteps marched across the bridge and into the night, Cade started laughing.

When Quinn scowled at him, Cade lifted an eyebrow. "If you two would marry—maybe have a baby or two to keep you in the same house—I could quit running over here in nothing but my boots and shorts. Lilian is out there, you know, just waiting to snag an unsuspecting bachelor."

"Now there's an idea—the living-together bit." Quinn watched the window in Maudie's bedroom light. "Why didn't I think of that?"

Cade stopped grinning, his expression stilling. "She's good for you, boyo. You're past that looking-like-hell stage." He nodded toward Quinn's new drawing board. "And you're drawing building plans again. That's what you were meant to do. That, and loving Tay."

"Tay brought me this and a kiss," Keely stated proudly as she danced through the open doorway of the mill at two o'clock the following afternoon. She turned around, modeling a wispy fairy gown with a wand and a crown. Quinn crouched by her, took one look at the satin bodice, the intricate hand-stitched sequins and gold dust, and knew that the costume cost more than he could afford.

"Tay made this for me. It's the first thing she ever sewed, Daddy," Keely exclaimed with delight, and turned again, smoothing the gauzy skirt lovingly. "She sewed it by hand, every night while she was away. She has a special little basket for her sewing things, and she put my drawings in her briefcase— Sometimes, when she's flying way high in the sky, she sewed my dress and thought of me, Daddy! She showed other people in the planes my pictures, and they said I could draw good. See my shoes?"

Keely propped her foot on Quinn's thigh and touched them with a sparkling wand. "Tay and me made these today. We glued stuff from old broken necklaces on 'em. They're my magic wand and dancing shoes."

"Now you look like a real fairy princess," Quinn said, his heart lurching as Taylor walked into the mill, dressed in jeans and a T-shirt. He kissed Keely, meeting Taylor's stormy dark stare. He recognized a showdown when he saw one, and he stood slowly. "Why don't you go show Grandma? Call her first, okay?"

Keely concentrated on dialing. Then she said excitedly, "Grandma, Tay is home. I'm coming to show you what she brought me, okay?" When she hung up, she ran to the door and paused. "Are you coming, Tay?"

"No, honey. I want to talk to your daddy," Taylor murmured with a smile. "I'll see you tomorrow for tea. You can have the very first taste of my scented geranium cake."

When Keely was gone, Taylor studied Quinn. "You look different."

"I'm dry."

"You're a proud man, Donovan. Too proud." She slapped a file against his chest. When he took it, she glanced down at the holes in his paint-stained jeans. "You still need a wardrobe. Open the file."

He placed it on his drawing table. "More investigation?"

"I'm a detail person, Quinn. A good one. When the questions don't have answers, I start digging." She nodded to the file. "That's interesting reading, Quinn. Try it," she said, turning around to leave.

He caught her arms, dragging her back to him. "I didn't want to care again, Tay. You've been gone for two months, damn you. I had plans. Now here you are, messing with things that you shouldn't."

A shadow of pain slid across her face. "Your designs weren't faulty, Quinn. Your wife bribed the inspector to overlook the poor-quality substitution."

"Hell, I know that."

"The design had been altered, too. Your... wife created a diversion until the changes were concealed. The combination sent that office building into the pavement, not your work. So you made a trade-off with your wife—you took the blame in your business partnership, you took Keely and you walked away from everything you built."

Quinn closed his eyes, fighting the nausea of the living nightmare. He released Taylor, turning away from her and running his fingers through his hair. "You might as well know everything. Nancy was having an affair with a junior partner before she became pregnant with Keely. We'd always wanted the same thing—but she wanted more and faster."

He shuddered, memories pushing at him, opening the old wounds. "The marriage was dead by that time, but Nancy wanted a fresh start. I was working too hard, leaving pieces of myself in every new project. Back then, I thought if she wanted a baby to make things right, then—" He inhaled as pain knifed through him. "It was a wrong decision. The reconciliation went wrong, and by that time, Nancy was pregnant and hating the baby. Me, too."

Taylor's hand touched his taut shoulder, soothing it. Her arms came around from behind, and she held him, leaning her face against his back. She rocked him gently, cradling him in her arms. "Quinn. Tell me everything. Let me in."

He closed his eyes, fighting the pain. "Or what? You'll investigate more?"

"What would you do if someone you loved was tearing himself apart?" she whispered against his back. "What would you do, Quinn, if you wanted a dream to last forever?"

His hands closed over hers, gripping her fingers. "You hurt me, Tay."

"Yes," she whispered unevenly, her arms tightening. "I'm sorry, Quinn. I love you so much…. I just want all of you, not the pieces. Please let me in, sweetheart."

Holding her hands tightly, Quinn stared out at the quiet lake. "What did you find?" he asked rawly.

"That your designs were perfect, dynamic and creative. That your wife tampered with materials, your designs, and bribed foremen and an inspector. That you took a bad beating and still took care of an infant daughter."

Quinn ignored the damp heat behind his lids and found he had drawn Taylor's hand over his rapidly beating heart.

"I had little choice. I took Keely, worked at home and created several sets of plans for the same company to get off their legal hook. When they were okayed, I ran with my daughter. It was all handled very quietly, professionally. Nancy had legally signed Keely over to me by that time in exchange for everything…and, of course, I took full blame for the changed design and agreed never to duplicate the designs that had become my signature."

"You have Keely and a talent…and you have me. Everyone needs a healing time. Dreams last forever. Yours are still there, waiting for you."

Quinn clamped his lips together, struggling through the pain, aware that the tears that he had held for years slid down his cheeks. "A syndicate was involved, selling under-quality materials. They threatened to…to hurt Keely. I knew that with Nancy's help, they could make it possible. I wasn't prepared to take that chance."

Locked to his back, Taylor held her breath. "Oh, Quinn…you're not a failure. You did what you had to do."

He brought her hand to his mouth, kissing the palm. She closed her fingers over the spot, locking her fist over his heart. Quinn closed his eyes and allowed himself to lean against her.

Against his back, Taylor whispered, "You've given me so much, and now I want it all. You're mine, Quinn Donovan."

"I am?" He smiled gently, rubbing his back against her softness. "Then you'll have to marry me, won't you?"

She stilled, then stepped back. Quinn turned, caught her hands and held them behind her back. He put his heart, his dreams, into the long kiss. "Welcome home, Tay darlin'," he whispered against her mouth.

"Quinn…we need to negotiate," she whispered unsteadily when she stepped back from him a moment later.

He stroked a fingertip down her hot cheek. "Fine."

Keely burst through the doorway with Digger. She looked at Taylor's face and Quinn's, studied the way they held each other loosely, then cheered. "Yeah! My leprechaun worked! He promised me a mommy, and I'm getting Tay!"

She touched the wand to Digger's head. He promptly tried to chew on it. "Let that be a lesson to you, my fair prince. Dreams and wishes do come true."

Quinn inhaled, strangled the flower bouquet in his fist and checked the shine on his boots. He smiled tightly, remembering Keely's excitement over Taylor's return and the way she'd puckered her mouth to draw enough moisture to spit at his boots. A man could teach his daughter old-fashioned ways, and putting a spit shine on boots was one of them.

Taylor swept open the door before he could knock. "Don't hover out there, Quinn. Come in," she said, stepping aside to let him enter.

He lifted an eyebrow, taking his time entering the parlor. "Is this how you negotiate? By throwing out orders?"

"Let us not begin our conference with torments," Taylor said loftily, straightening her red cotton sweater. The dark shade matched her slacks and the red polish on her bare toes. "I thought we would discuss our…problem…in a way that I understand and deal with more easily. A business conference may not be the usual way that—" She stopped talking when Quinn thrust the flowers at her, then bent to kiss her slowly.

She tasted of chocolate frosting, of rainbows and sunshine, and of promises. He dived into the tastes, treasuring each one.

"Tay," he whispered when she stared at him blankly, "I need you." He kissed her again to let her know how much.

"Need me?" she repeated slowly, her eyes focusing on him.

He curved his hand around her nape, massaged the tight cords for a moment, then drew her against him.

"You fit so perfectly," he whispered against her hair, inhaling the cool and exotic scent.

"I fit?" Then, slowly she whispered, "Donovan, you can't just walk in here and ruin my conference. I have a schedule planned, an agenda ... dinner ... dessert ... negotiations ... a settlement ... my work ... your talent ..."

"Okay. Fine," he said, taking the bouquet from between them. He tossed it to a table and held her closer. He rocked her against him and nuzzled her hair, smiling when he realized that Taylor was holding him very tightly.

"Keeping to a schedule is important," Taylor said firmly against his chest.

"Okay." Quinn kissed the side of her cheek, her eyes. He feared she would move away, and he counted the heartbeats when she sighed against his throat, holding him nearer. "We missed you. I missed you and Keely missed you. The rest of Blarney Flats missed you, too."

"Mmm." She kissed the side of his throat, allowing him to rock her, to smooth the line of her back.

He slid his hand under her sweater, stroking her skin. His heart raced as he asked a question he had promised not to press— "Did you mean it when you said you loved me, Tay?"

She tensed in his arms, and Quinn feared that she would move away. "Yes. I meant it," she whispered unevenly, a century later. "I've never said that to another person...except Keely...and Digger."

"Then it looks like I'm headed for a lifetime of keeping you in line. You shot the hell out of my plans, Tay darlin'," Quinn whispered, unbuttoning her sweater slowly.

She watched his hands as they unsnapped her front-hooked bra. "I did? How?"

He caressed her breasts, cherishing them, and watched her eyes darken the way he hoped they would for a lifetime. "Tay darlin', a man wants to come after his ladylove. To court her and have a tidy little bankroll in his pocket—" He thought of the new contracts from people who discovered he was creating again, the excitement racing through him again....

"But, Quinn, you have given me so much. You've given me tenderness and love and laughter and dreams."

He drew her against him gently. He eased her closer to him, and Taylor locked her arms around him tightly. Quinn swayed with her, his heart filling with love. He kissed her temple, nuzzling his way down to her throat. "I love you, Tay darlin'," he whispered. "You're my heart. You've made me complete."

"Oh, Quinn..." Taylor lifted her head drawing his mouth down to hers. The kiss was long and sweet and gentle, and when she drew away, she ran a fingertip across Quinn's damp lashes. "You're a loving man, Donovan, but you're ruining my schedule. I wanted to have my way with you. Then while you were under my spell, I wanted to lay out the terms of our life together. I had issues, and negotiations—like a baby sister for Keely and how to remodel this house, putting in your studio and my office...and who would stay home while the other travels... and then I wanted to make you pay for not calling me once in two months...."

Quinn thought of the thousand times he'd grabbed the telephone, of the hundred times he'd planned to walk into her office, kissing her senseless and telling her he loved her. He thought of the hours lying sleepless, needing her. Then he thought of the excitement he wanted to share with Taylor when his first plan sold, and the second, and the third—

"Fine," he said simply, scooping her up in his arms and hurrying up the stairs while she laughed.

When dawn rose over Ferguson Lake the next morning, Taylor leaned her back against Quinn's chest as they sat on the dock. Framed by his arms and legs, her hand resting on his thigh and his arms holding her, she wished time would stop. "We're naked under this sheet," she whispered drowsily as he tucked it closer around them.

Quinn smoothed her foot with his and nuzzled her cheek. Taylor lifted her hand to caress his rough jaw. "I think Baby likes us here. Quinn, darling..." She tested the new en-

dearment, then changed to "Sweetheart, why do you think
Keely stopped asking me when I was coming back?"

Quinn's rough, warm hand fitted over her breast, caressing it gently. "Mmm... Could have something to do with
her finding her leprechaun... or rather a tiny little voice reassuring her that you were coming back and she would have
her wish."

Taylor looked up at him, cherishing his rugged, un-
shaven, untamed, rawly masculine smirk. "How?"

He inhaled the morning air, gathering her closer. "A re-
mote-control tape recorder does wonders. Especially when
it's under a prime leprechaun bush. I was desperate after a
week of missing you. After two weeks, I knew I was coming after you... so it seemed logical to ease Keely's wor-
ries."

"You beast..." Taylor laughed up at him, just as he
started to make growling noises and nuzzle her throat.

He eased down on the dock and spread himself over her.
"A very hungry beast who loves you."

"Quinn, not again—not here," she exclaimed, giggling
and squirming as he slid under the sheet to rummage down
the length of her body. He nibbled and kissed his way back
up, emerging from the sheet looking tousled and delectable.

Then Quinn was leaning over her, his eyes filled with love.
Taylor nestled beneath his weight, drawing the sheet around
them. "Love," she said simply, realizing she had truly come
home.

"You fill my heart," Quinn whispered softly just as an
enormous splash sounded in the dark waters.

"Shush, Baby..." Taylor ordered quietly, gathering
Quinn closer. "Go back to sleep."

Epilogue

"Hell, no." Quinn glared at Taylor as a bright orange oak leaf fell between them. The entire population of Blarney Flats had attended their October wedding, and Keely had acted as flower girl. Now, after the church wedding, at which Taylor wore the classic, long white bridal gown, Quinn held her hand while they cut the tall, layered cake. He licked away the frosting from the piece she had placed in his mouth and scowled down at her set expression. "No. You won't give Maudie's land and the lake to the town as your dowry. It's enough that we'll be living in your house."

She forced a tight smile. "Quinn, dear. This is our wedding day. Your family is here. I thought the announcement would please you."

"Yes," Cade agreed, lifting his mug of beer in a toast and grinning. "Quinn Daniel, be pleased and behave yourself."

Taylor blew away her bridal veil, which was fluttering along her cheek. She pushed another piece of cake into Quinn's mouth. "I've made up my mind. You gave me that lovely bridal chest, Quinn. A dowry is customary in Blarney Flats. If you act like a chauvinistic—''

She took another deep breath and smiled while people took wedding pictures of the happy bride and groom. She began again, ''If you throw a hissy fit now, Quinn Donovan...the wedding is off.''

He smiled smugly. ''We're already married, Tay darlin'. You said your I-do's. I've got you. You're mine.''

''Oh...well, then...if I can't give my bridal dowry, you can stay at the millhouse. I'll give the land and the lake anyway.''

''Donovan, she's got you beat,'' Moriarity murmured. ''In another minute she'll be tossing the wedding cake at you.''

''Sure livens things up with you two deciding to live here,'' Lyle Flynn tossed in.

''Okay, let's negotiate. It's the men-only hour—or rather two hours, Quinn darling...or the land as my dowry. Take it or leave it.''

''Quinn. Do something,'' Moriarity said quickly, fear creeping into his tone.

''That's blackmail,'' Quinn said, bending to lick away the frosting clinging to her bottom lip. ''If I'm staying at the millhouse, so can my wife.''

Taylor tilted her head, kissed him softly, then sucked slightly on his bottom lip. ''Too bad, Quinn darling. Give over, boyo. I want to give the land to the people Maudie loved. She would have loved the land as my dowry, just as much as I love you.''

He smiled at her with the love that would last until eternity. ''Fine.''

''Thank God, the men-only hour is saved.'' Moriarity cheered with the other men, but Quinn was walking away from the church, carrying his bride.

Two years later, Quinn leaned against the post on Maudie's front porch and watched Keely bounce down the steps wearing her brand-new first-grade clothes. Digger howled unhappily from the back porch, wanting to follow at Keely's heels as usual.

Keely stopped on the walkway, looking back at Quinn. His daughter grinned widely as Taylor came out the front door. "Bye, Mommy. When I get home, I'll tell you everything that happened."

"I'll be waiting. I love you," Taylor called, leaning against Quinn's back and wrapping her arms around him.

He placed his hands over hers, smoothing the plain wide band. "I love you, too. Bye, Daddy. Don't let Digger be sad, okay? I'll play with him when I get home," Keely called, swinging her new book bag.

Quinn inhaled, fighting his emotions, then Taylor's hand slid to rest on his heart. "Come on, Daddy, don't be sad," she whispered against his bare shoulder, then kissed it. "She's only going to school."

"She was a baby just a minute ago," Quinn protested as Taylor began to sway slightly. The brushing of her soft, full breasts eased the small pain of his daughter growing up.

Taylor nuzzled his back, leaning her cheek against him. "Our schedule is working out nicely, don't you think? My job as a consultant works in with your schedule. When one of us has to travel, the other is home, and neither one of us has been gone very long. Oh, Quinn, I'm so happy. I've got the family I've always wanted...."

Quinn watched another little girl dressed in brand-new first-grade clothes join Keely. His career was growing now, the new blueprints for an office building in a nearby town almost complete. His plans for Blarney's new city hall were drawing attention from other builders.

Their lives were filled with love, though Taylor still had dark moments when she fought her early trauma. Quinn inhaled the fragrant air and leaned back slightly against his wife.

Taylor had fought him every inch, but in the end, he'd worn her down and she'd faced the shadows of her family with him. After meeting the Harts, he wondered how that bloodless clan could have produced Taylor. Still, it was a shadow that they had faced together, and Taylor had cried for hours afterward.

Taylor kissed his shoulder, and he turned his head to kiss her slowly, softly. She had made his life complete, delighting him at every turn, fighting with him and holding her own in the midst of Blarney Flats. The danger to the men only hour was never far away. Taylor kissed him again, lingeringly, and he tasted her hunger. "So, boyo, we have two choices of what to do this first school morning—"

He leaned back, luxuriating in Taylor's new softness. With proper meals and rest, she had gained a little weight which made the game of dragon and elves even more interesting. "Two choices, Tay? Could one be making euphoric love?" he teased.

"Euphoric? Quinn, there are times when you can be quite the heated savage."

"Only trying to come up to your standards, Tay darlin'."

"Hmm... A bit of euphoric lovemaking would be perfect. But first, why don't we walk down to the dock and reassure Baby that Keely will be just fine?"

Quinn turned and bent to kiss Taylor properly. "I love you, Tay. You are my life."

"And I love you," she returned, nestling closer. "By the way, boyo, did I tell you that you're going to be a daddy again? Better start brushing up on your fairy-dusting techniques."

* * * * *

Take 4 bestselling love stories FREE

Plus get a FREE surprise gift!

Special Limited-time Offer

Mail to Silhouette Reader Service™

3010 Walden Avenue
P.O. Box 1867
Buffalo, N.Y. 14269-1867

YES! Please send me 4 free Silhouette Desire® novels and my free surprise gift. Then send me 6 brand-new novels every month, which I will receive months before they appear in bookstores. Bill me at the low price of $2.44 each plus 25¢ delivery and applicable sales tax, if any.* That's the complete price and—compared to the cover prices of $2.99 each—quite a bargain! I understand that accepting the books and gift places me under no obligation ever to buy any books. I can always return a shipment and cancel at any time. Even if I never buy another book from Silhouette, the 4 free books and the surprise gift are mine to keep forever.

225 BPA ANRS

Name _____ (PLEASE PRINT)

Address _____ Apt. No. _____

City _____ State _____ Zip _____

This offer is limited to one order per household and not valid to present Silhouette Desire® subscribers. *Terms and prices are subject to change without notice.
Sales tax applicable in N.Y.

UDES-94R

©1990 Harlequin Enterprises Limited

MONTANA
Mavericks

Stories that capture living and loving beneath the Big Sky, where legends live on...and the mystery is just beginning.

This September, look for

THE WIDOW AND THE RODEO MAN
by Jackie Merritt

And don't miss a minute of the loving as the mystery continues with:

SLEEPING WITH THE ENEMY
by Myrna Temte (October)
THE ONCE AND FUTURE WIFE
by Laurie Paige (November)
THE RANCHER TAKES A WIFE
by Jackie Merritt (December),
and many more!

Wait, there's more! Win a trip to a Montana mountain resort. For details, look for this month's MONTANA MAVERICKS title at your favorite retail outlet.

Only from ᵀᴹ **Silhouette®** where passion lives.

The Loop™

Is the future what it's cracked up to be?

This September, tune in to see why Jessica's partying days are over in

GETTING IT RIGHT: JESSICA
by Carla Cassidy

She had flunked out of college and nearly out of life. Her father expected her to come crawling home, and her friends expected her to fall off the wagon...but Jessica decided she'd rather sell her soul before she screwed up again. So she squeezed into an apartment with some girls she barely knew, got a job that barely paid the bills and decided that things were looking up. Trouble was, no one knew better than her that *looks* could be deceiving.

The ups and downs of modern life continue with

GETTING REAL: CHRISTOPHER
by Kathryn Jensen in October

GETTING PERSONAL: BECKY
by Janet Quin Harkin in November

Get smart. Get into "The Loop!"

JINGLE BELLS, WEDDING BELLS:
Silhouette's Christmas Collection for 1994

Christmas Wish List

*To beat the crowds at the malls and get the perfect present for *everyone,* even that snoopy Mrs. Smith next door!

*To get through the holiday parties without running my panty hose.

*To bake cookies, decorate the house and serve the perfect Christmas dinner—just like the women in all those magazines.

*To sit down, curl up and read my Silhouette Christmas stories!

Join *New York Times* bestselling author Nora Roberts, along with popular writers Barbara Boswell, Myrna Temte and Elizabeth August, as we celebrate the joys of Christmas—and the magic of marriage—with

JINGLE BELLS, WEDDING BELLS

Silhouette's Christmas Collection for 1994.

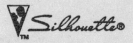

JBWB

Coming in September from Joan Johnston

CHILDREN OF

Remember the Whitelaws of Texas from Joan Johnston's bestselling series *Hawk's Way?* Well, they settled down to have three sweet and innocent little kids. Now those little Whitelaws are all grown up—and not so innocent! And Silhouette Desire has captured their stories in a very sexy miniseries—*Children of Hawk's Way.*

Why is gorgeous rancher Falcon Whitelaw marrying a widowed mother who'd rather sleep with a rattlesnake than him?

Find out in Book One, *The Unforgiving Bride* (SD #878), coming your way this September...only from

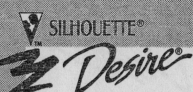
SILHOUETTE®

Desire®

MAN of the Month

1994

They're the hottest books around...with heroes you've grown to know—and *love*....

Created by top authors— the ones *you* say are your favorites....

Don't miss a single one of these handsome hunks—

In July **Wolfe Watching** by **Joan Hohl**	In October **Temptation Texas Style!** by **Annette Broadrick**
In August **Fusion** by **Cait London**	In November **The Accidental Bridegroom** by **Ann Major**
In September **Family Feud** by **Barbara Boswell**	In December **An Obsolete Man** by **Lass Small**

Man of the Month...only from Silhouette Desire

MOM94JD